MURDER IN THE PARK

THE HIGHLAND PARK MURDERS

T. Lloyd Hardwick

I

MURDER IN THE PARK
THE HIGHLAND PARK MURDERS

MAYS PRINTING COMPANY, Inc.
15800 Livernois Avenue - Detroit, Michigan 48238
(313) 861-1900 - A Certified Minority Printer
www.MaysPrinting.com

Printed in the United States of America

ACKNOWLEDGEMENT

THE ALL

III

Chapter 1

Mona offered little resistance as Leo pressed his face toward her soft, sensuous lips and planted a long, wet kiss that sent her spiraling into a state of euphoria. The kiss was abruptly disturbed, however, by the harsh pounding on her apartment door by Highland Park police detectives.

Leo was all too familiar with the sound of pounding flesh and bones on creaky wooden doors. So much so that his natural instincts had at least one of his funny-shaped legs on Mona's second-floor fire escape before the pounding stopped. Raw fear and adrenaline carried the rest of his small frame down the heavily rusted escape ladder, right down to busy, bustling Woodward Avenue, where he made his way into an old raggedy Dodge Duster.

Leo knew that if the police stopped him for any reason at all, he would go directly to jail for outstanding arrest warrants; he would do just about anything to avoid that. He drove his fear and busted vehicle into the dark of the city night.

Mona finally opened the door of her stale, cramped apartment to two slightly agitated police detectives in dark blue suits. They were on a routine door-to-door interview process of all the tenants, compliments of the stuffy old perverted building superintendent.

Mona let the oddly paired men enter her apartment virtually unchallenged only briefly flashing what appeared to be legitimate identification.

The first detective to speak was Henly, a 20-year veteran of the force who, at first glance, appeared to be one cheeseburger away from a massive heart attack. The morbidly obese detective smelled of cheap cologne and the old greasy spoon restaurant that the men had visited less than an hour before coming to Mona's building.

The sweat-drenched detective hastily loosened his tie as he scanned the small apartment with his highly trained eyes, almost simultaneously.

Detective Henly asked Mona if she had heard any strange noises coming from the abandoned building adjacent to her rundown apartment building between the hours of 12 a.m. and 7 a.m. He nodded in the direction of his partner, Jinn, who keenly observed the scene.

Jinn presented a stark contrast to Henley's very existence. His frame was extremely thin, and he was well groomed. His well educated profile and ultra-quiet manner made him highly suited for the role of a good cop every time.

The seemingly tranquil detective was barely 40 years old; yet he possessed the instinct of a pedigreed hunting dog that always caught the scent of its prey. This same instinct led Detective Jinn directly over to the slightly cracked window that overlooked the busy avenue below.

The detective's next question was as obvious as the rising of the morning sun. Who was it that left Mona's apartment in such a hurry? And why did that person use the fire escape for a quick exit?

Mona had no choice but to give some sort of explanation, seeing that her table was playing host to two long-stemmed glasses half filled with cheap red wine and an ashtray with two types of freshly extinguished cigarettes nestled in their respective holders.

She told the inquisitive detectives that her brother had made the speedy exit down the fire escape to avoid being arrested for delinquent child support payments. In reality, her brother had been dead for more than five years.

This little crafting of words was designed to divert the detectives' attention long enough for her to move from the shabby tenement after they left the building. Mona herself was trying to avoid arrest warrants in Oakland

and Macomb counties for check fraud and high-end shoplifting.

The seasoned detectives could sense a lie in a fly. Detective Jinn gave his partner a certain look of suspicion as he quietly took down the false information. The fat man's eyebrows rose to arched peaks as he led the way out of the rancid apartment with his prim and proper partner in tow.

Leo had every reason to fear being arrested by police. He was the Highland Park serial killer fresh from a bloody slaughter that had not been performed in his usual trademark MO. Leo was covered from head to toe with the blood of his fifth victim.

He preferred death by strangulation. This intense act of overpowering his victims and strangling them to death was as sexually arousing for Leo as it was for a man wrestling on the floor with a woman as a prelude to their foreplay.

Leo had a special place reserved where he could clean up and lay low in relative privacy, a place left to him by his dear, deceased grandmother. He usually rested up for a couple of weeks between killings. This time, it would be even longer, due to the time needed to heal from his stab wounds.

3At first, it seemed that his victim had gotten the upper hand on the veteran killer with the knife she carried in her tall black suede go-go boots. The naked woman rolled off of her right side and stabbed Leo in the upper chest, far from any vital organs.

There was nothing sexual about the murder of Leo's fifth victim. It was pure, uninhibited rage that possessed this evil killer. He broke his right thumb while crushing his victim's skull with a heavy piece of concrete used to break the windows out of the abandoned house by the mischievous youth in the neighborhood. The crushing blow rendered his victim unrecognizable as a human being.

The body was discovered by cadaver dogs after nearby residents complained of an all too familiar odor of rotting flesh and decomposing body fluids that had permeated the air of Highland Park for nearly two years.

Chapter 2

All of the preceding carnage was taking place a few short miles from the house owned by Mona's family. She was her mother's favorite child, and so was Sirus, Tarralyn, Nolan, and Jayla, the baby of the bunch. As an unspoken rule of society, the youngest child always appeared to get away with more shit than their older siblings.

Jayla lived an alternate lifestyle to the rest of the family. Let's keep it real; Jayla was as gay as a newly sprouted blade of grass in the springtime, and she didn't care who knew it. She had been in and out of relationships with older women since her days as a high school student.

Jayla was just 16 years old when she fell in love with her Phys. Ed. teacher, Mrs. Noelle Bowman, who had been a college basketball star in the 80s when she performed plenty of fancy moves on and off the court. Noelle had played the position of point guard for as along as she could remember. She could move the ball up and down the court with the best of them.

She had all the right moves. As a high school coach, she was also known for putting the moves on young, impressionable female students long after the bell rang.

The coach was separated from her verbally abusive husband of five years, and with good reason. Coach Noelle Bowman continued to live the lifestyle that brought about many problems in her marriage in the first place.

Jayla was primed and ready by the time Noelle put the moves on her. The first time was after the coach drove her home in the pouring rain following a practice session. She had already rented a suite at the Dearborn Hyatt Regency, after her husband attempted to break into the house that the estranged couple once shared.

At the Hyatt Regency, the seemingly innocent high school student, Jayla Reed, rocked the tube socks off her 6' high school gym teacher, who was completely in love with her young student from that point on.

Jayla was the giver in the bedroom, which always gave her the upper hand. She made sure her lovers were satisfied long before she could fully enjoy her share of the action.

Noelle had come from an affluent Chicago family, so Jayla pretty much got whatever she wanted, and she wanted it all!

Once, when the couple was out celebrating after Jayla's senior awards ceremony, Noelle's estranged husband drove up and scared the living daylights out of the unsuspecting lovers, first by cutting them off with his car at a stop sign, and then erratically waving his gun at them.

Mr. Bowman fired two shots into the air, just as he sped off into the dusk, laughing aloud in a devilishly insane manner.

Meanwhile, Leo's wounds had nearly healed and his urge to kill was kindling, like choice wood chips in a fancy fireplace, crackling and giving off the heat of evil deeds with every flicker of the flames.

Victim #6 was scheduled to meet her fate on the damp, cold basement floor of a burned-out and abandoned Highland Park home. Though the home had been torched months earlier, the distinctive stench of charred wood still lingered in the gentle, moist breezes of the mild spring evening that traveled for blocks.

The desolate habitat didn't discourage Leo in the least. It only assured him that not many people would be venturing into his potential kill zone. Most nights, Leo would sleep in the places he selected to kill his victims the night before, absorbing his surroundings and masturbating to the thoughts of a vicious struggle and eventual kill. After the explosion, Leo would lay in his semen until he was completely satisfied within.

Carmen Deil was a 31-year-old mother of three and an admitted prostitute and drug addict, much like Leo's previous victims. She decided to turn one more trick that night; it turned out to be the last john she would ever serve.

Try to imagine, if you will, that death had just set its sights on you, and you were the primary target of the moment. All that you did from that time forward were the last things you would do on this earthly plane. Now imagine your last conversation, your last argument, your last cigarette, your last struggle, and ultimately your last breath.

Carmen Deil, black female, 5' tall, 98 pounds, lay dead and naked on her back, clothed only by the glow of moonlight reflecting on her lifeless body. It was as if she was participating in a photo opportunity.

Her eyes were fixed in a dead stare at the stars above, peering through the large, gaping hole in the roof, forged by the fires of days gone by. Leo had raped and strangled Carmen with less effort than he exerted on any of his previous victims, due to her small stature, but victim #6 was no less satisfying than his very first kill.

A steady flow of semen ran down Leo's legs while he proceeded to remove the life force from his petite victim. He never wore underwear during the commission of his crimes. He didn't want any type of restraints hindering him from reaching the fullness of his climax.

The night proved to be very successful for the 5'6" serial killer…and unsuccessful for the feuding agencies involved in the cases. The Highland Park Police, Michigan State Police, and the Detroit Police Department were all conducting separate investigations, none sharing vital information with the other agencies. It was no wonder the killings continued.

Chapter 3

Mona was experiencing a certain level of success of her own in those days. She had scored a boatload of stolen goods and clothing along with her brother, Sirus, her driver. The thieving siblings gave the local malls pure hell. Mona always stashed her goods at the house of her girlfriend, Farrah.

Farrah was game for whatever Mona was into at the time. Just as it was when Mona lost her virginity; Farrah was literally in the next bed with another boy, imitating her every sound and move. Needless to say, Farrah lost her virginity as well.

During Farrah's early years in high school, her parents were either hard at work or busy traveling the globe, leaving her to quite literally raise herself in the large, fully restored two-family flat.

Sirus and Farrah had gotten it on once or twice in the past. Now, the two could not stand one another. They kept the peace around Mona, for the sake of the friendship, however. All the merchandise stolen the night before had been sold by noon the next day, and oh! What a good day it was for the crew. Farrah took her cut in the clothing, while Sirus headed straight for the crack house on Clairmount and the Lodge, and Mona went off in search of a new place to live.

Just as Mona was standing in front of the beauty supply store on Grand River and Joy Road, thinking of the passionate kiss she had shared with

Leo in her rundown apartment on Woodward Avenue, he approached her from behind, using his hands to gently blindfold her and speaking softly the words, "Guess who?" Mona's heart was pounding a mile a minute.

She immediately recognized Leo's soft, sultry voice and flung her shapely body around and into his muscular arms, returning the kiss they shared only months earlier. There was something about Mona that intrigued Leo to no end.

Leo viewed most of the women he encountered as whores and junkies that he once paid to get him off. He now became their judge, jury, and executioner. His fascination with Mona was probably what kept her alive. It didn't take much for Mona to hop her sexy ass into Leo's old, beat-up ride in the parking lot.

The two headed over to Mr. FoFo's Deli for lunch and a quick conversation before departing for the day. Mona returned to Mama Reed's house to an ongoing discussion that spanned more than 30 years.

Tarralyn, Mona's older sister, was believed to be emotionally fragile, dating back to when she was a child. Mona and Tarralyn were sexually abused as children by their father, Terrance Reed. Not only did he physically abuse them, he also left them tormented by the fact that Mama Reed refused to believe them or confront her pedophile husband about her daughters' accusations of abuse.

Mona entered the kitchen just as her baby sister, Jayla, was comforting Tarralyn at the kitchen table. Tarralyn suddenly stood up and began to shout at the top of her voice, "Why didn't Mama do something?"

At that very moment, Mama Reed walked in on her daughters with their arms interlocked in a huddle-like position. "What the hell is going on in here?" she shouted.

Tarralyn was the first to lift her head and break away from the huddle. Her eyes were bloodshot red, and her inner fires kindled at the sound of her mother's voice.

"Don't be bringin' up that old shit in my house, girl!" thundered Mama Reed.

Tarralyn froze in her tracks, as her fires were suddenly tempered by the raging waters of her mother's words. Her mindset quickly reverted to that of a child, as Mama Reed ordered the 45-year-old woman to go to her room. Tarralyn waltzed off as though she were still a child, much to the shock and dismay of her sisters.

They looked at each other and simultaneously voiced their words in perfect harmony, "Why do you treat her like that?" It was Mona's turn to shout the sentiments that her big sister was not allowed to express. Mona always stood her ground when it came to defending herself.

Being molested was a forbidden subject in the Reed family household when they were growing up. Mama Reed had drummed her husband's innocence into her daughters' heads so much that the girls began to doubt their own stories over the years.

Discussions on the subject of abuse were just as forbidden as the sacred apple of the Garden was for Adam and Eve to eat. But Mona was about to bite that sacred apple and spurt the juices of truth all over the kitchen walls.

"Daddy raped us, Mama," shouted Mona in an angry voice. "And you didn't do anything to stop him."

Mama Reed stood glued in her tracks with a glass of water firmly clutched in her right hand. Her mind drifted back to the first time she witnessed her drunken husband fondling her then perfectly normal eight-year-old daughter, Tarralyn.

Mama Reed had put the young girl to bed after her bath. She then moseyed off to bed shortly thereafter. She later walked in on her husband with his pants and underwear well below his ashy ankles, and his eight-year-old daughter seated on his lap with her long white cotton nightgown raised high above her tiny waist.

Terrance Reed had fathered another family on Detroit's East Side that Mama Reed only later discovered after his untimely death. What she didn't know was that her husband had fathered two children with his long-time girlfriend's oldest daughter and had molested her younger girls on numerous occasions.

Mama Reed suddenly realized that she had drifted off to the past after her glass went crashing down, sending glass shards and water all over the kitchen floor. Now she was upset to the point where she slammed the dish rack full of her good dishes to the floor, adding to the already dangerous debris accumulating on the newly installed ceramic tiles.

"I did the best I could for my children," she screamed.

That statement would be the last Mona would hear from her mother for months.

Chapter 4

Jayla cried aloud as she cleaned up the kitchen in the aftermath of the Reed family explosion. Mona, on the other hand, gathered her things in a large travel bag and made her way over to Farrah's house, where she was always welcome, until her apartment was completed.

The Reed family was about to be hit by a devastating revelation: the horrific loss of a close family member, and a debilitating illness that threatened to bring total ruination to the family. Highland Park detectives had made their way over to Mama Reed's house on Pingree Street between the Lodge Freeway and Woodrow Wilson Street.

Detectives Jinn and Henly's knocks were a tad bit less aggressive than those of their visit to Mona's old apartment. They were following up on the lie Mona had given them during their initial questioning of all the residents of her building.

Jayla opened the door to what appeared to be the oddest looking pair of men she had ever seen. Detective Jinn was a dark black-skinned, slim built, wall-eyed, celebrated homicide dick, who took a no-nonsense approach to his police work, and he almost always caught his man. He was feared throughout the city by criminals and cops alike.

Jayla knew immediately that they were cops simply by their authoritative postures. Well, at least for one of the detectives, it was painfully obvious. Detroit Detective Henly didn't bother to wait for Jayla's greeting; he got straight to the point. He was definitely suited for the role of bad-ass cop.

"Does Mona Reed reside here?"

Jayla turned her back to the detectives waiting on the other side of the screen door and shouted for her mother with no regard for the question the detective just asked her.

Mama Reed approached the door in her quilted day robe and matching slippers, not knowing why the detectives were at her door. She asked them in a cautious and humble tone what their business was at her home. Mama Reed was no stranger to police visits to her address when her younger son, Nolan, was alive. He stayed in more trouble than the mob.

With Terrance Reed dead from a mysterious stabbing in the alley a few houses from their home, there was no one to help redirect his teenaged son's aggressive behavior.

Nolan grew up fast and furious with the streets as his teacher and guns and knives as his toys. He even tried his hand at hustling and was beat and shot to death one month after opening a new drug house above a party store on Hamilton and Highland Street.

Mama Reed was strangely relieved after hearing the detectives ask for her daughter by name. She herself had been harboring a huge secret that placed her on the edge every time someone knocked on her door.

The detectives were allowed to enter the Reed household only after Detective Merten arrived with a search warrant and additional officers for the task. Detectives from Detroit and Highland Park searched Mama Reed's house from top to bottom, to no avail.

Mona hadn't seen her mother in nearly two months, not since the big family blow-up.

Jayla and her mother were shown an artist's sketch of the man Mona's building superintendent described the night they also spoke to Mona after the latest murder took place in the abandoned building next door. The sketch bore an uncanny resemblance to the serial killer, Leo Adams.

Neither of the detective agencies realized how very close they were to an actual identity of the man who had held two cities in mortal terror for the past several months. They still needed to speak to Mona as soon as possible to clear her mystery visitor who made a quick exit.

Detective Jinn applied only mild pressure when asking his questions. It appeared that the detectives left empty handed, but Jinn had managed to slip the Reed's phone bill into the inner breast pocket of his suit without being noticed by the nervous women.

Later at the station over freshly brewed black coffee and the mandatory glazed and powdered doughnuts, the detectives split up the numbers on the phone bills and retrieved addresses for all of them. They concentrated on the more frequently used numbers first, and then on the others.

Mona and Farrah had the most calls on the listing; thus, it was off to Farrah's two-family flat off of Linwood Avenue.

T. LLOYD HARDWICK

Chapter 5

Mona was sharp as shit in her off-white Saks Fifth Avenue pants suit. She strolled confidently up Philadelphia Street with the posture of a runway model, ambling past the beautiful well-kept brick structures that once housed an entire Jewish community in the early 1900s and that now gave most people a sense of nostalgia. Detective Henly's family once owned property on the very same block.

Just as Mona began her ascent to the front porch, the detectives hurried up the street from their unmarked car and startled her. "You're under arrest, Ms. Reed," Detective Henly blurted out.

Mona was now under arrest and on her way to jail for grand larceny and, more importantly, to answer questions about her elusive house guest. Detroit Police held Mona for three days, asking about the man described by the apartment superintendent.

When they got no further than when they first questioned Mona, the frustrated detectives turned her over to Oakland and Macomb counties for outstanding arrest warrants. Mama Reed mortgaged one of her properties to use as bail money to free her daughter.

Mona was fresh out of jail, but not out of trouble, by far. She now had cases pending in Wayne, Oakland, and Macomb counties, all bearing down on her at once. She began to drink as a result of her depression, just as things were about to go from bad to worse.

Farrah was already getting high off of crack cocaine with Mona's brother, Sirus. He had inched his way back into Farrah's life; first, with weed, and then with alcohol, and eventually, with crack cocaine. It was only a matter of time before Mona would take her first trip to Crackville, U. S. A. The usually strong Mona Reed had become weak and vulnerable in her time of troubles.

Despite all that was going on, Jayla was enjoying a certain level of success in her relationship with her former Phys. Ed. teacher, Noelle Bowman. She and Jayla were completely in love with each other and had moved into a two-bedroom apartment on Evergreen Road in Southfield.

Jayla was 20 years old when she left her mother's house for good. She and Noelle had become quite the item around the gay club circuit. Once on a late night outing, they were pulled over by Detroit police after the couple ran a red light in the gay district at Woodward and McNichols.

Officers approached the vehicle in their usual precautionary manner. The officer approaching the passenger side of the vehicle recognized Noelle as the ex-wife of his former partner, Benny Bowman, who was now his supervisor.

The officer radioed his supervisor with the information, who in turn rushed over to the scene and personally searched Noelle's car with total impunity. The ladies were scantily dressed and high as a couple of kites…and greatly irritated at the way they were being treated by police.

Jayla's youthful rebellion and drunken outbursts were about to get her cute little half-naked ass tossed into a jail cell for the night. After all, she had been driving drunk when she ran the light. Noelle never uttered a word.

Sergeant Benny Bowman detained his ex-wife and her lover long enough to gather the necessary information he needed to further his harassment, all within the legal realm of his police duties, of course. Jayla and Noelle were finally allowed to leave with only a small traffic infraction.

Sergeant Bowman now had his ex-wife's vehicle make and model and her new address and apartment number. He followed his ex-wife from place to place for weeks until he memorized her schedule.

The obsessed sergeant was about to throw it all away…his career, his beautiful new fiancée, and quite frankly, his life. It seemed that every time the good sergeant was in the presence of his ex-wife, his demons only allowed him the thoughts of his former wife choosing women over his love for her.

This fact infuriated him down to his very soul. Sergeant Bowman not only harbored the deep thoughts of hatred for his ex-wife in the recesses of his heart; he also had actually developed a plan of killing Noelle, just before she dropped out of sight nearly three years earlier.

The plan to kill Noelle was obviously dwelling on the surface of his mind the night that he waited outside Mama Reed's house with a one-gallon milk jug filled with gasoline and two semi-automatic weapons on his passenger seat. He was parked and waiting to unleash the years of anger and aggression.

Sergeant Bowman took the safety feature off both his weapons and slipped them into his belted denim pants. He then watched the women exit the house, kissing and touching each other intimately as they entered their vehicle. The ladies continued their intimate exchanges in the car completely unaware of the danger that lurked in their midst.

Pop...pop...pop...pop was the sound that filled the air for a two-block radius. Benny Bowman fired four fatal shots that carried him across the border of no return. The very sight of Noelle kissing her lover was just enough to tip the scale of anger and not allow him to leave the ladies alive a moment longer.

In his sick, distorted mind, he had just killed his worst enemy, an enemy that had plagued his very thought process for far too long.

He had shot the women twice each in nearly identical places on their bodies: once in the left temple and once in the chest. Death was instantaneous! He then casually doused the dead women with the entire gallon of gasoline and set them ablaze.

He stood by the raging flames as if he were at a bonfire at a camp outing. Benny Bowman appeared completely unaffected by the blazing fire that had engulfed the entire vehicle at that point.

The gunshots failed to yield the usual attention expected of shots ringing out in a neighborhood filled with children and elders. But the enormous blaze was just too much to ignore. It was the blinding glow of the flames and the blaring sound of approaching fire trucks that lured Mama Reed's ailing body to the front window, where she discovered her neighbors gathered on the sidewalk and on their neatly manicured lawns staring in the direction of her home.

Just a quick adjustment of her eyes revealed the unimaginable horrors of a burning vehicle in her driveway that sent her elderly body barreling swiftly down the wooden staircase of her home. A mother's instinct sent Mama Reed charging toward the vehicle that revealed two motionless human figures burning in the flames.

"My baby! My baby!" screamed Mama Reed, just before passing out unconscious in the arms of a slim, clean-shaven fireman. Mama Reed was transported to Henry Ford Hospital for observation.

In all the excitement, Benny Bowman managed to ease his stolen van up the street, virtually undetected. He drove the van downriver and dumped it in a field of trash and construction debris. It would be several months before he would be brought to justice.

Chapter 6

Nearly two days went by before Mona and Sirus received the news of Jayla's tragic death and their mother's subsequent hospitalization. Mama Reed suffered a mild stroke the night of the tragic murders.

The very sight of his mother in such a condition drove Sirus right out of the hospital and back to the family house where he searched for money to feed his drug habit.

Mona could barely keep it together herself. All of the anger she felt for her mother had been replaced by an overwhelming sadness and concern for her life. Mona's almond-shaped eyes cried a river beside her mother's bed.

Sirus reached out to the local crack dealers to aid him in easing his pain in time of need.

Farrah was totally strung out and under Sirus's control. She begged, borrowed, and stole anything she could get her hands on to keep her man happy.

Meanwhile, Leo Adams decided to scout out another kill zone for his next victim just a few blocks across the border in the city of Detroit, where he had been reluctant to do business. Woodward Avenue seemed to be prime hunting ground for the small-framed merciless killer, but it would be Hamilton Avenue that would generate the brutal killer's next two victims.

Though Woodward Avenue was well known for its wide assortment of hookers, it wasn't the only place in town that had hoes. Besides, a change of venue was very necessary for Leo to evade capture by the massive man-hunt and police sting operations that were being carried out in his honor.

Leo parked his old Duster several blocks from the designated kill zone and approached his victims on foot, first flashing a small wad of money and then his trademark smile of perfectly straight teeth; thereby luring his wayward victims to their last moments of life on earth.

Leo felt that he was doing the world a huge favor by ridding the plan-et of what he called, "junky whore scum of the earth." He had recently explored several new potential kill zones along Hamilton Avenue to serve his purpose.

He seemed to lean more toward old burned-out houses with structural integrity so fragile as to be vulnerable to a strong gust of wind that would scatter it hither and yon.

Leo would later learn that he had a special connection to his next vic-tim, Porsha Freeman. She would stroll her 29-year-old muscularly athletic body up and down Hamilton Avenue in search of cash to pay for her drugs and lodging. Porsha was a bit of a loner, who hadn't been around her fam-ily in a couple of years.

She claimed the small stretch of road from Chicago Blvd. as far as Six Mile Road as her own domain in search of johns to fulfill her needs. Porsha was once a budding high school track star with tremendous potential and a host of colleges and universities vying for her attendance. She gave it all up for a guy who used to kick her in the ass from sunup to sundown, just for sport. Imagine that!

Leo chose an abandoned apartment building on Webb and Hamilton that had recently played host to a crime scene filled with old empty crack packets, wall-to-wall trash, and a plethora of old syringes randomly sprawled about the ground level apartment, which was accessible only from the rear of the building. The John Doe found in the building was given a hot shot of drugs to keep him from ever speaking to the police as an informant.

The building seemed like a prime place for a kill. Leo performed his usual night before ritual of masturbating in anticipation of a kill. His nature began to rise as he visualized strangling his previous victim to death.

He became so excited in his thrill that he stood up and flung his narrow body into the partially exposed wood wall and began to moan like a wounded animal as he ejaculated a hefty portion of semen down the wall and onto the floor. And this was just a practice run!

Chapter 7

The next night, Leo maneuvered in and out of the shadows of Hamilton Avenue with the stealth of a cat. His heart was beating faster and faster, as he inched his way from Glendale to Highland Avenue and then onto Webb Street, where he found the 5'7" Porsha Freeman cursing and fussing out her last john for God only knows what.

Leo waited across the street at the Hamilton bus stop in front of the Roofing Supply Company with the patience of a professional hunter.

Most nights, it took Porsha an hour or so between johns. This night she would have to wait for only five minutes before her last john of the night.

Leo's eyes widened and his heart began to flutter out of control. And, his nature became harder than the ground on which he stood. He was now operating on the toxic body fluid known to the world as adrenaline. The moments before a kill were as close to a natural high as Leo had ever come. His nature slowly dripped pre-seminal fluids in the same fashion of an oozing maple tree yielding sap.

As Leo cruised across the street, all he could hear was the soft, gentle, almost child-like voice of Porsha Freeman saying, "Come on, baby, let me make you feel good." If Leo hadn't seen her speak directly to him, he would have sworn the voice came from another woman.

Porsha had just shaken off the sting of her last john's perverted request of a porno-styled S&M beating, topped off with a golden shower over his open wounds. There she stood: the tall, dark, once popular high school track star totally unaware that she was staring death directly in the eye.

All Porsha could think of was her next high. She was all legs. It was hard even for a sadistic killer like Leo not to notice the anatomical crafts-manship of this one-time beauty. There was no time for admiration. It was a time to kill.

The two waltzed off arm in arm as though they were longtime lovers. Porsha was no stranger to the darkened corridors that led to the many chambers of death and degradation. A dim reflection of a leaning, aging street light was all that shone into the darkened room that she settled on.

Leo allowed her to lead him to her own personal kill zone. At this point, what difference would it make? She attempted to kiss him directly on his lips, much to his resistance. She then slid an old sofa pillow over with her right foot, directly in front of Leo's Converse All-Stars, and dropped rough-ly to her knees, latching onto Leo's zipper as she nestled into her paid posi-tion.

Porsha gently pulled out Leo's 12-inch staff to begin her work. In a sen-sually laden tone, she whispered, "Oooh, baby, we're about to have lots of fun with this!" She then placed her small lips around the huge throbbing head of Leo's penis and took a pull on it, as if she was puffing a Cuban cigar.

That's when Leo delivered a brutal punch to Porsha's face that caught her completely off guard. The harsh blow knocked the shapely legged woman onto her back; with his limp rod still swinging from his pants and with the swiftness of a feline creature, Leo pounced on what was to become his next murder victim…Victim #6.

Porsha was barely cognizant of her surroundings and hardly able to utter a word. In her mind, she was cursing Leo's very birth, but her lips could only whisper a half word at a time.

"Shut up, bitch!" thundered Leo.

As the effects of the devastating punch began to wear off, Porsha began the final struggle of her life. Her wildly resistant arms only temporarily staved off Leo's attempt to remove her life. He had no choice but to deliver a menacing right hand blow that rendered Porsha as still as a log.

He stripped off every inch of her clothing and parted her legs as he straddled her naked frame and proceeded to remove her last breaths by the brutal act of strangulation. Leo's penis was still out of his pants from Porsha's early attempt to bring him pleasure.

His semen burst forth, finding its way all over Porsha's neck and upper torso. Her eyes reflected the terror of a horrible death, as she lay nude with the semen of her killer running down both sides of her inanimate body.

Leo stuffed his limp staff back into his pants and made haste out of the building the same way he had entered.

Chapter 8

The Detroit and Highland Park police were all over the area the next day, after a junkie discovered the body just before his routine shoot-up (getting high). Detectives Jinn and Merten promptly arrived at the scene of the crime and immediately recognized the M.O. of their elusive killer.

Detective Jinn sat outside Farrah's place for weeks, hoping that Mona would receive a visit from the same mystery man. Needless to say, the stake-out was a total bust.

Leo continued to operate 10 steps ahead of federal, state, and local law enforcement agencies. The physical evidence was overwhelming at the scene of nearly every one of Leo's kills. Dried semen, body hairs, and of course, death by strangulation had become the calling card of this merciless killer.

All the law enforcement agencies involved in the case were about to receive a major break with the formation of the new federal task force that pooled all the information from all the agencies into one centralized system of checks and balances.

Meanwhile, Detroit and Highland Park police were still not sharing vital information and the flurry of incoming tips that would assist them in the common goal of capturing one of the country's most elusive serial killers.

The inter-agency rifts kept a brutal killer on the streets far longer than he should have been. The FBI sent two special agents to organize the established information profile of the killer and form the inter-agency task force that would take the stone-cold killer off of the streets once and for all.

Among all the tips and confusion was the report of a confessed prostitute and crack addict, known as Dierdra Holmes, who would later become the single most important witness in the entire investigation.

She was the only victim to escape the deadly clutches of the man she called Lee. Dierdra fought Lee with every inch of her being on the dirt and glass-covered floor of the old Howard Johnson restaurant before barely escaping nude and terrified with multiple lacerations on her legs and back. Dierdra had simply out-maneuvered Lee, whose dropped pants prevented him from stealing her life.

Two other victims had met their fate in the abandoned Monterey Motel, adjacent to that restaurant. After hearing of the two bodies discovered in that motel, Dierdra was compelled to come forward with her story. She ran into the streets flagging down Wayne County Sheriff's mounted patrolman, Dilbert Clayton, to share her near-death experience.

Dierdra's performance in the middle of the street nearly spooked the deputy's horse into the oncoming Woodward Avenue traffic. Trooper Clayton guided his horse to safety and far out of reach of the boisterous and hysterical woman. The trooper then climbed down off his horse to hear Dierdra's complaint. He cautiously approached the screaming woman, instructing her to calm down.

"His name is Lee. His name is Lee," shouted Dierdra hysterically.

"Who are you talking about, ma'am?" asked the trooper in a calm voice.

"The killer's name is Lee. He tried to kill me last month!" she cried.

Trooper Clayton radioed for a squad car to pick Dierdra up from his Highland Park location and take her to the State Police Command Post at Sixth and Howard Street, directly across from the Greyhound Bus Terminal.

News of Dierdra's arrival traveled through the state building faster than a lean turd down a vacuum-flush toilet system. She was to be treated with the utmost regard, no matter how absurd her story sounded.

As it turned out, her story carried more weight than a fat man cheating on his second day of dieting. Dierdra told the state police about her drug addiction, her near-death experience, and most importantly her attacker's description.

She described the man she called Lee to a tee! State police now had a very good likeness of Leo Adams on paper to circulate throughout the community and state.

While all of this was taking place, the feds were forming a joint-agency task force to share all relative information concerning the case.

Chapter 9

Acting on the information they received from their only living witness and on the shared information of the joint agencies, the newly formed task force launched a door-to-door search for their suspect with a detailed description in hand.

Just as the task force was completing weeks of searching door to door, police received a call of a man, fitting the description of the suspect, Lee, and a woman entering an abandoned house just off of Hamilton Avenue. All four law enforcement agencies cordoned off a three-block radius of the area in question. The early morning raid was like something out of the movies.

The task force wasn't about to allow their suspect to slip through their fingers. The SWAT team awaited word from their commander to enter the house and take down the vicious killer.

"Go, go, go, go!" shouted the SWAT team leader, as the men kicked into action, first ripping the rusted armored gate off its hinges and then kicking in the cheap aluminum door on their first attempt.

The team spread out in search of their suspect, who hadn't heard a sound at this point of the intrusion. He and the alleged prostitute were in the uppermost part of the house, the attic.

Once the SWAT team finally entered the suspect's personal dwelling space, they discovered wall-to-wall debris that one would expect to find in any back alley of America. There was trash, beer cans, and cheap liquor bottles, all sprawled about amidst what appeared to be the naked bodies of two lifeless souls.

With his sight locked on the principal suspect, the SWAT team member rushed forward in one smooth motion and dragged the female away from the suspect. The rest of the team swarmed on suspect Lee with their weapons on hot, ready to end it all.

Team members were shouting a variety of commands at their suspect to get him to stand up. The SWAT team then handcuffed the groggy suspect and carted him off to jail in a convoy of vehicles that was reminiscent of a presidential motorcade.

The news media had broadcast the arrest of the Highland Park serial killer across the country before the suspect had been fingerprinted and processed. The only thing left for the task force to do was to positively identify the man known only as Lee by the sole surviving witness, Dierdra Holmes.

She had been under federal protection ever since her claim of escape from the man she continued to call Lee. Dierdra was tucked away at a secret location in Dearborn, Michigan, until the capture of the man she claimed as the killer and her attacker.

Now, it was time to show and prove. Dierdra was whisked back to Detroit in a matter of minutes. The energy and anticipation at the federal building was incredible, to say the least. And, of course, the Highland Park police were on cloud nine due to the fact that their office had received the lead on the house where the suspect was arrested. Nonetheless, it would be a huge payoff for all of the agencies involved.

Chapter 10

Dierdra walked into the dimly lit room and sat on a cold metal chair just as nervous as a child on her first day of school. At least four agents hovered over her shoulder, as the lights on the other side of the two-way mirror suddenly began to illuminate the area specifically designed for criminal line-ups and witness identification.

The men began to file in and take their place in front of the numbers and stand against the wall to designate their correct height. Once the men were in position facing the glass, one of the agents asked Dierdra if any of the men behind the glass was her attacker.

Dierdra stood up and shouted, "That's not him!"

The feds were floored by her words. They were sure that they had the right man in custody. The news media rushed to retract their claims of the capture of Highland Park's elusive serial killer.

The man that the feds had in custody was, in fact, Leon Bradley, a drug addict who had been caught with a girlfriend who was a prostitute and thief. This wrongful arrest was a setback within itself. Now the task force was ultra-cautious about the many tips that continued to pour into their offices.

While the federal task force was bogged down with bogus tips and the wrongful arrest, Detroit police detectives were about to cast a net of their own to catch police sergeant, Benny Bowman, for the heinous murder of his ex-wife, Noelle, and her lover, Jayla Reed.

If you recall, Bowman shot both women to death as they sat in the Reed family driveway just before setting them ablaze with a gallon of gasoline and, along with the rest of the neighborhood, watching them char. The crazed sergeant then casually drove off into the night before the fire department finished its job.

Police detectives had been wire-tapping the sergeant's phone line for quite some time in hopes of a confession. Bowman finally broke down and set himself free by telling his aging mother of his horrific sins in a sad and tearful telephone confession that sealed his fate.

Due to Bowman's popularity as a good cop, the initial investigation became stagnated until orders from the top brass threatened certain careers, after which the wiretaps were ordered on the sergeant's phone line, which lead to his confession, capture, and eventual conviction.

Mama Reed shed a single tear onto her sad round face as her daughter, Mona, shared the news of Bowman's capture and conviction. Mona now divided her time between getting high and caring for her ailing mother. Mama Reed's condition had worsened in recent months, and she began preparing herself for the trip to the Great Beyond.

Later than night, she summoned her two surviving daughters into her room for a talk. It seemed as if she had regained her full strength as she sat up in her sick bed and explained how and why she murdered their father in the street as he walked home in his usual drunken stupor.

Mama Reed had stabbed Terrance in a fit of rage until the knife broke off in his chest. Mona was completely blown away by her mother's confession! Tarralyn just stood there with a fixed, frozen smirk on her face that was indicative of a mischievous child that just struck the cookie jar without getting caught.

It was at that very moment that Mona fell to her knees, sobbing uncontrollably. She wondered how she could have been born into such a dysfunctional family.

The women finally emerged from their mother's room and headed for the respective rooms where they were raised as children. Mona was mentally exhausted as she drifted further into dreamland. Her subconscience had her firmly in its grips in a matter of seconds, as she envisioned herself being carried off on a bed of soft white rose petals while wearing a long, flowing white satin nightgown that trailed along the path of an extensive corridor, appearing to release the fragrant rose petals along the way.

The long corridor led Mona to a single set of tall white French doors that slowly opened as she drifted closer and closer. In the haze of the mist-filled room was a beautifully adorned, bright red sarcophagus that sat in the center of the rotunda-shaped room.

Mona's white rose petal ride stopped within ten feet of the bright red casket. She felt a strange comfort come over her as if she belonged in this mysterious setting. She took only nine of the 10 steps toward the casket, and from one foot away she beheld an elderly woman with the likeness of her mother.

Mona's heart began to flutter as she moved closer to the lifeless body. Her eyes began to shed tiny drops of sunlight onto the woman's face that slowly reanimated the old lifeless form, long enough to utter the words, "Momma's gonna be all right."

Mona suddenly sprang from her sleep to find herself fully dressed in her same clothing. She quickly shook off the remainder of her sleep and ran down the hall to her mother's room and burst through the doorway to find Tarralyn curled up alongside her mother's lifeless body that had expired during the night.

Mona stood calm as she dialed EMS. She gently sat in the high-back chair and patiently awaited their arrival.

Dorothy "Mama" Reed was laid to rest alongside her daughter, Jayla, and son, Nolan, at the Woodlawn Estates Cemetery where they would rest together for all eternity.

Chapter 11

Mona slowly began her descent into a world of drug use, theft, and prostitution. She had become used to taking to the streets to feed her drug habit, but she mainly serviced a steady flow of johns at Farrah's two-family flat. Farrah even had a few plant workers that she serviced on a regular basis.

This arrangement suited Sirus's lazy ass just fine. Between Farrah's johns and Mona's hustles, Sirus never had to leave the house for drugs. Mona was so fed up with Sirus's bullshit that she decided to strike out on her own.

As dangerous as it was out there, Mona had become comfortable with turning a few tricks a day. A few tricks turned into a few more, and before she knew it, she was servicing johns damn near around the clock, or at least when her habit called her to put in some quick overtime. Mona was too busy getting high to notice that Sirus had supplanted himself as guardian over the affairs of his sister, Tarralyn, and their mother's estate.

Sirus then placed Tarralyn in an adult foster care system paid for by the state. Now, with no one to challenge him, Sirus first mortgaged the family home at a quick loan agency that had a reputation for predatory lending in the vast urban areas across America. Needless to say, Sirus never even attempted to make the first payment on the loan; thus, the house went into foreclosure in a matter of months.

Over the next few months, Sirus went from one sleazy motel to the next, parading his nickel whores and his newly found wealth like a classic ghetto superstar on a break from a busy Hollywood schedule. And it wouldn't be long before he would draw the attention of other shady characters looking to cash in on his new wealth.

Late one night at a boulevard motel, Sirus was shot, robbed, and left for dead. Had it not been for his neighbors calling the police and the hospital being a few short blocks away, Sirus would've been a done deal.

While Sirus was busy recovering from his wounds, Leo was busy driving law enforcement out of their minds with his latest double murders that were somewhat out of character for the country's most wanted killer. It had become painfully obvious that Leo was now taunting the task force by just randomly killing Victim #7 and Victim #8 in such a brutal fashion that it almost appeared to be the work of another killer.

However, the professionally trained eyes of the feds recognized Leo's handiwork, despite his attempts to throw them off. Some say Leo was getting sloppy; others said he was pissing in the feds' faces.

Whatever the case, the murder toll reached an alarming eight count with no end in sight. The search continued, and so did the murders. Leo felt his celebrity status increasing daily. He was basking in his own glory, knowing full well a massive hunt was underway to remove him from the streets.

Police were unsure of Leo's work on the badly decomposed body of a prostitute found in Chet's old and abandoned gun shop on Hamilton Avenue. Nevertheless, the body count was at a staggering nine, with only a composite sketch of a possible suspect circulating around the entire state of Michigan.

Detectives Jinn and Merten would meet with Dierdra Holmes a couple of times a week to cruise the streets in search of their suspect. Both detectives alternated their personal vehicles in pursuit of the elusive killer. Not knowing the results of this simple method of operation would eventually yield them the biggest fish of all, Leo Adams, but not before the killer went full circle to where the detectives first picked up his scent.

Mona had been arrested several times for prostitution and petty theft, but the short stints in local precincts did nothing to curb her urge to get high. It wasn't until the night she bumped into an old friend from her past that she decided to seek help for her drug problem.

That old friend was Leo Adams, someone Mona had secretly fallen for nearly a year and a half earlier. She only knew Leo's soft and gentle side, as did most of the people he encountered by day, but the nights brought out one of the most vicious killers this country would ever know.

Mona had hit rock bottom by the time she ran into Leo in front of King Cole's Supermarket, where she was trying to pick up her first john of the day to satisfy her morning jones (urge).

Leo was staggeringly disappointed in the only woman left in the world that he respected. Imagine the irony in that shit!

Mona's face lit up like a kid in a toy store, while Leo's countenance was quite the opposite. He literally had to catch his breath and calm himself down before talking to her about her life and troubles. He walked Mona around the corner to Mr. FoFo's Deli, where the two had once shared a memorable lunch on a sunny afternoon.

Leo made Mona promise that she would get help right away. He also gave her a 50-dollar bill and jokingly threatened to kill her if he ever caught her selling her body on the streets again. Mona checked into a local rehab center two days later.

T. LLOYD HARDWICK

Chapter 12

While Mona was beginning her drug rehabilitation therapy, Leo was starting to feel that devilish urge to kill burning deep within his being. He resorted to his old method of scouting out his kill zone for his next victim. Detroit seemed like a fitting place for what police initially thought was Leo's final victim.

This had to be a very special kill for Leo. Even he felt that his killing days were numbered. He also wanted his victim to be special, as well. And special she was!

The sadistic killer chose Darcy Owens, a well liked, well loved registered nurse at the Brookdale Nursing and Convalescent Center on Woodward and Atkinson Street, adjacent to the gas station on the corner of Clairmount Avenue.

Before the killings began, Darcy would catch the Woodward bus down to her New Center apartment complex without a second thought, but the murders were too overwhelming in the nightly news to ignore. She therefore decided to walk up one full block under the watchful eye of the nursing home security guard to her sister's house and wait for her faithful boyfriend to end his shift and pick her up for the night.

The security guard wasn't the only one watching Darcy. Leo watched the nurse for an entire week. He even jumped through the six-foot tall hedge that surrounded the property to test his escape route.

Leo chose the darkest area of the property to strike his victim. The night guard made a habit of walking the nurses out of the building to their cars. In Darcy's case, he would watch her walk the full block of Atkinson before looking after the other nurses going home. This gave Nurse Darcy a sense of security that the other nurses weren't privy to.

On this particular night, a slight deviation in the regular program was about to result in the death of Victim #10 for the evil killer. The night guard's boss was ringing the phone at the guard station just as Darcy was about to leave the building for the night.

She gestured to the tall man that she would be all right. Nothing was further from the truth. The night guard had no choice but to answer the phone. His boss and job were on the line for two tardy days in a two-week period.

It is interesting how certain small combinations of events intersect to cause such great catastrophes and horrors in and around the world. One simple phone call made the difference between life and death for Darcy Owens.

Leo watched the door of the nursing home as Darcy exited alone. He leaped out of the hedges like a ferocious beast attacking his helpless prey. He quickly disabled his victim with a rear chokehold, while swiftly pulling her into the hedges to do his final damage. He removed every stitch of Nurse Darcey's clothing, as well as her life, while bursting forth his poisonous venom all over her nude, lifeless body.

The city of Detroit was in an uproar over the murder of Darcy Owens, and the police department was feeling the full brunt of the mayor's office.

As the manhunt continued, Mona celebrated her last two days in the Sobriety House facility with her thoughts as her only company. The reality of her past deeds was rearing its ugly head, despite all that she had been taught in rehab classes on how to handle the overwhelming urges to get high.

The fact is that the human mind constantly seeks those things that bring it pleasure and delight, and tends to avoid those things that cause it harm. Mona was experiencing a plethora of emotions, combined with traces of anxiety and outright fear of leaving her new comfort zone.

All of these were simply post-program jitters. It was as if the next night acted as a healing ointment that raised all of her troubling thoughts to the surface of her very being, allowing the coming of the gentle morning breeze to sweep them up and carry them out into the atmosphere.

Mona arose from her slumber confident, agile and ready for the challenges of the world outside. Her first stop was the popular Woodlawn Estates Cemetery, where her mother, brother, and sister were buried. She promised herself that she would not shed a single tear on that sacred burial ground of her loved ones.

It was her inner being, however, that forced a single tear to the surface of her kind face and evaporated in the soothing westward breeze. Mona had finally made her peace with the death of her loved ones.

She next made her way back to her taxi and gently requested the driver to "just drive." She eventually forwarded directions to her extremely patient driver to the Normandie Hotel on Woodward Avenue. She secured enough food and snacks to last a couple of days to keep her off the streets. The rehab program had rented the room for Mona for one month until she found a steady job.

Her day was both mentally and physically exhausting. She barely had enough energy to bathe her beautiful limbs in the bubble-filled tub of water she drew with thoughts of a Calgon moment. She slid into the steaming hot water as she clenched her teeth, barely able to stand the heat.

The soothing water sent thoughts racing towards the southern portion of her body. The combination of scented candles and soothing water provoked an erotic sensation that streaked through her body like an electrical charge.

Mona was as horny as hell by the time she climbed out of the tub and onto the quilted double bedspread, where she lay naked as the day she was born. Her entire body was covered with water droplets. She hadn't the faintest memory of the last time she experienced an orgasm with or without a man's help.

One flick of the remote changed Mona's thoughts of a fantasy orgasm into reality. The hotel's 24-hour closed circuit porn channels were about to aid in her journey into sexual wonderland.

Mona slowly rubbed a combination of rose-scented lotion and baby oil, first on her sensuous tender breasts and then on her lower limbs, giving her genitalia a bit more attention than the rest of her extremities. She glanced occasionally at the television.

She now had both hands planted firmly between her thighs, imitating as much of the porno flick as she could stand. Now, with her right index finger gently inserted in her vagina, she began to simulate a passionate slow grind with her perfectly round hips, leading to the grand finale. She was just seconds away from her goal of physical bliss.

What started as a fantasy ended in an incredible explosion within the sacred chambers of a very sane and sober Mona Reed.

Mona lay there basking in the afterglow of her sexual high, wondering if she had enough energy to do it all over again. That short pause gave way to a slight doze that spiraled into a deep sleep, a sleep that held her in its clutches into the wee hours of the morning.

She sprang from her sleep startled and frightened by the sound of crashing lamps and constant slams into the ultra thin walls of the adjacent apartment. In what her hazed conscience could surmise, it sounded like a hooker trying to escape the brutal clutches of an angry pimp, an all too familiar reminder of her former life.

Mona's eyes raced towards the makeshift barricade she had concocted upon entry into her small, but cozy dwelling. As her conscience reached its fullness, she realized that the sounds were coming from beyond her personal space.

Now, fully awake, she swung her shapely legs to the right side of the bed, suddenly realizing that her vaginal region still housed a fair amount of residual juices from her previous activities. She forged a smile for a reason only she knew. She quickly cleansed herself and dressed in a matter of minutes.

Chapter 13

It was now 4 a.m. and the streets were buzzing with the usual underworld characters that were typical of a Saturday night on Woodward Avenue. Mona felt the insatiable urge to smoke, but realized she was fresh out of cigarettes. She knew that the gas station on Harmon Street was just a five-minute walk from the Normandie Hotel, where she was housed temporarily.

She decided to go out for some smokes. She was wearing a cute little black blouse she lifted from Saks Fifth Avenue, along with some severely tight jeans that paraded her curvaceous figure to the max.

Mona had a natural stride that pissed off even the most professional hookers. It was a combination of strong, confident woman and highly experienced runway model. Her Max Toben heels added that extra "uhhh" to her model-like stride.

She could have easily blazed the runways of New York, Paris, and Milan, but this night, the world would have to be content with her burning up Woodward Avenue in search of single pack of Virginia Slims menthol to calm her nerves.

Mona was all too familiar with the risk that women faced at those hours of the morning trying to survive between fixes and johns. Her impending fears were quickly eradicated by that first long drag of smoke that seemed like the best damned cigarette in the world.

She stopped and gazed over at the working girls on the other side of the street milling about in their usual manner. She shuddered to think what her life would have become had she continued on such a destructive path. No less than six johns had tried their best to lure her into their cars with the promise of cash, drugs, and a good time.

Mona strolled north on Woodward in the direction of the Normandie. Just as she placed her right foot onto the gravel to cross Englewood Street, a little rusty car seemed to pull up out of nowhere, right up to the stop sign. Mona paid no mind, as the man honked his horn to gain her attention.

She finally gave a brief obligatory glance to make sure the driver of the car noticed her, for safety reasons. The driver stuck his head out of the window and shouted, "Long time, no see."

It was none other than Leo Adams! Mona could hardly contain herself at the sound of his voice. "Where you been, boy?" she shouted back in reply. "Pull over so we can talk."

Leo cleared his throat to stifle a chuckle at her request. He was still in the hunt mode and wasn't about to come down from that rare one-of-a-kind high, not even for an old friend like Mona.

Descriptions of Leo were all over town at this point. It was a matter of time before the authorities slapped a cold pair of cuffs on his wrists.

Leo briefly reflected on the day he discovered Mona selling her body on the same avenue where she now stood and how angry he had become, but his afterthoughts were that of how good Mona made him feel when they were alone.

"Get in, girl! Let's take a ride," urged Leo.

The thought barely had time to process before Mona was placing her sexy round hips in Leo's plaid-covered passenger seat. 204 Tuxedo Street was about to become the last kill zone Leo Adams would ever need, and Mona Reed was about to become Leo's final victim, #11.

Their conversation was as casual as two people out on a normal date, with one exception: this date was designed with death in mind.

Chapter 14

Leo flashed his famous smile as he pulled into the long driveway that led him to a partially leaning, weather-beaten garage. The fresh scent of jasmine and lilac filled the night air from the surrounding plants and trees in the backyard. It was in this very yard that Leo killed his first animal at the tender age of 12; by strangulation, of course.

Mona was joyfully surprised at how well kept Leo's house was. She even commented on how immaculately clean it was. Leo shrugged his shoulders as he led Mona into the den.

She sat patiently until he returned with two glasses half-filled with white wine. "I want to make love to you," Leo uttered softly.

Mona was slightly stunned by Leo's forwardness, but hesitant in her response. She too had longed for the deeply satisfying penetration of a man's penis, probably more than he wanted her. "We can do a little something, baby. I don't mind," she replied in her sexiest voice.

Leo walked over to his aging console hi-fi/stereo system, encased in an intricately carved cherry case that was the showpiece of the entire room. He then fingered through an extensive collection of vinyl LPs that rivaled that of any professional disc jockey. He finally selected the album that came to his mind only a moment earlier.

Major Harris' "Love Won't Make Me Wait" was the song that bounced off the acoustically capable den walls and into Mona's seemingly heated temple.

"Take another sip," chanted Leo in a soft voice.

Mona had just violated Rule #1 of her rehab program: Stay as far away from drugs and alcohol as possible. "Fuck it," murmured Mona beneath her breath. "One drink ain't never killed nobody," she reasoned to herself.

The sexually soothing song had reached its midpoint when Leo flashed his smile, robbing her of any other thoughts besides him.

Down on his knees in front of her, he began to loosen her pants. First the top button, then the zipper. He reached for her waist, firmly grasping her fancy rhinestone belt. With one swift yank, he deprived Mona of her pants, panties, and a few pubic hairs. She was fully exposed.

Mona was accustomed to a neatly trimmed pussy that never failed to excite the souls that were fortunate enough to enter her sacred temple. Leo was no exception. He nearly gasped at the sight of what appeared to be endless treasures.

The rose-scented lotion invaded Leo's nostrils at the speed of light, causing him to close his eyes and enjoy the moment for what it was. With his eyes closed, his nose advanced his face - and long tongue - towards Mona's honey pot. Her body had already prepared the perfect blend of fluids to ease the penetration of her intrusive lover.

Leo licked the slowly seeping juices from the surface of Mona's temple, just as if he were licking his favorite ice cream cone.

"Oh, shit," sighed Mona, as she nestled into the plastic-covered sofa. Leo ventured deeper and deeper into his endeavor, causing Mona to completely lose herself in the moment. He then placed both of his hands directly behind her legs in the fold of her knees, raising both legs simultaneously, thus flinging wide open the doors to her sacred temple.

Leo quickly fixed his wide lips around Mona's clitoris with the furiousness of a lion on its prey. Mona had just left the planet and was en route to a place beyond the stars. It was a grand explosion, which was visibly evident by the fluid rushing down Leo's chin.

Shortly thereafter, Mona felt certain dizziness come over her that just wouldn't subside. At first, she thought it was the effect of the wine, combined with her powerful climax; when, in fact, it was the powerful effect of a date rape drug beginning to overpower her senses.

Leo suddenly disappeared into the haze that clouded her vision. At this point, the lighting in the den became psychedelic, an odyssey that lasted all of two minutes before Mona passed out with her legs extended toward both ends of the sofa.

T. LLOYD HARDWICK

Chapter 15

Two and a half hours later, Leo decided to wake his captive lover to the pungent odor of smelling salts and an angry voice shouting, "Wake up, bitch! You are about to die!"

Mona's eyes widened as far as her lids would allow. She appeared fully awake, but barely cognizant of Leo's true intentions toward her. As she regained her vision, she noticed Leo, stark naked, standing next to a blazing wood-burning fireplace.

He mischievously prodded the fire with the poker iron, as he reflected on his days as a young lad searching for places to hide, while his mother turned tricks in the family home. Often, Leo would watch her activities from the gaping hole in the floor, where it seemed like his mother stared directly at him as she performed her paid duties. Other times, he would just hide in the closet adjacent to his mother's room.

The sounds were all the same to young Leo's ears. It sounded like the men were harming his mother; when, in fact, his mother was a screamer in the bedroom. To a child, that's hard to distinguish. One thing Leo was very sure of was the night his loving mother was brutally murdered in their Highland Park home.

Leo's rage began to kindle with every thought of his mother's brutal murder. She had been very kind to him, and that was what prompted his initial attraction to Mona Reed. She reminded Leo of his tender, loving mother. That's the reason he had not killed her before now.

Leo moved closer to his grandmother's four-poster bed, where he had gagged Mona and tied her outstretched arms and legs, after which he brandished the red hot, glowing tip of the poker iron. As one can imagine, Mona managed a muffled scream that fell on deaf ears.

Leo came closer as Mona's tearing eyes appeared to bulge out of her head. She was in a state of sheer terror.

Mona's thoughts began to probe her mind for the reason Leo had suddenly flipped out on her. He gestured a lunge with the hot poker within inches of Mona's left eye. She struggled against her restraints, to no avail. He jumped from the bed, repeating the words, "You gotta die, bitch! You gotta die!"

He placed the poker back in the fire and quickly darted from the room. Mona's eyes checked out the room and looked at her restraints for a possible escape.

Leo ran his naked ass up the floral-carpeted stairway to the room directly above the room where his naked prisoner was bound. He then slid aside the small Oriental rug that covered the hole that gave him a clear view of his struggling captive.

Leo's dick began to rise to the occasion, as Mona attempted to free herself from the intricately tied ropes. Leo leaned forward with his fully erect staff in hand, peering through the hole at Mona's terror. The excitement of her struggle was so overwhelming that he began to wildly ejaculate an enormous amount of semen onto the carpet, as he squirmed around like a fish out of water.

In an instant, Leo appeared out of nowhere. He had straddled atop Mona in the same fashion he had assumed with so many of the other women. He slowly removed the large blue bandana he had used to gag Mona, and ordered her to not say a word.

Salty tears steadily flowed down the sides of Mona's high-boned cheeks, as she completely ignored Leo's orders. "Why are you treating me like this?" she pleaded.

Leo slapped her so hard her mouth began to bleed. Her teeth were blood-soaked, and her body began to tremble. Leo wanted Mona to struggle so that he could maximize the thrill of his kill. When that didn't work, he untied her hands and feet to allow her the opportunity to run free.

Mona sat up as Leo rose to his feet. Both were completely nude. Leo's breathing pattern began to intensify as his heart rate shifted into high gear.

He was hell-bent on having a knock-down, drag-out struggle with Mona, even if he had to create one himself. He wanted her to run, so he could chase her down, and then as she was kicking and screaming he would remove her precious life.

Mona ran as fast as she could to the fireplace, where she grabbed the cold poker from its propped position. Leo's eyes bulged and his staff quickly erected at the mere sight of Mona's all-out aggression.

Her mind and body were in full battle mode, a battle for her very life. Leo faked a move toward Mona, which in turn provoked a batter-like swing of the poker that nearly tore Leo's jaw off the hinges. He became so excited that he prematurely fired off a round of semen that sent him bending over, clutching his penis and allowing Mona the opportunity to strike the killer across his left shoulder, a blow that sent him and his squirting pipe forcefully to the floor.

Mona dashed towards the door as quickly as she could move. Leo quickly recovered from his fall and sprang to his feet with flaming rage in his eyes. He now wanted to put an end to this little charade as soon as possible.

He pounced on Mona, knocking the poker to the floor and striking her in the face with a devastating right cross. The brutal punch was effective enough to send Mona tumbling to the floor, but not enough to render her unconscious.

Leo was finally about to get his wish of a ferocious struggle. He was also about to release the fullness of his fury, as well. Mona struggled for her life as her attacker straddled her, forcing his agenda of death upon her.

Mona literally scratched the living skin off of Leo to expose his filthy flesh to the world. He fought through Mona's struggle until he was able to place his hands around her long, beautiful neck and proceed to the final phase of his deadly task. He pressed harder and harder on Mona's windpipe, until her bloodshot eyes reached the full extent of their sockets and her long arms ceased to struggle.

Chapter 16

Mona Cherie Reed, Leo's 11th and final victim, lay dead from strangulation on an old Oriental rug at the entranceway of the serial killer's door. Something about this kill was unsettling to Leo. He felt strangely uncomfortable as he rushed to shower and dress.

Leo stared at Mona's lifeless body for a complete hour, before rolling her up in the large rug and carrying her to the basement, where he carefully placed her in an old deep freezer until he figured out how to dispose of the body. Leo was weak and exhausted. He had only enough energy to carry himself over to the plastic-covered sofa, where he slept for several hours.

An entire week had gone by since Mona's brutal death, and Leo still hadn't left his lair of lethal activity. Convinced that the killer was a resident of Highland Park, Detectives Jinn and Merten continued to search the very streets where the killer had made his name.

On one such occasion, after picking up Leo's only surviving witness, Dierdra Holmes, the persistence of the detectives was about to pay off. Most serial killers don't just stop killing, because it's the right thing to do. They stop killing only when they're caught. And Leo's urge to kill again was brewing like a fresh pot of hot morning coffee.

As Leo prepared to hunt for his next victim, Dierdra and her detective companions prepared to scour even the darkest alleys in search of the killer. Leo bounced in and out of the cracks and crevices of the night in search of a victim.

This particular night, the detectives decided to extent their search to the direction of the Cass corridor area. Just as Detective Jinn was about to turn off of the Chrysler service drive onto Cass Avenue, Dierdra began to shout, "That's him! That's Lee, damn it!"

The detectives weren't taking any chances. Jinn rolled the vehicle onto the sidewalk, blocking a surprised Leo Adams from a quick escape.

The oversized Detective Merten leaped from the vehicle with his gun drawn and ordered Dierdra to stay in the car. Jinn made his way over to the suspect with the police sketch in one hand and his service revolver in the other.

By that time, Dierdra had made her way up close to the detectives. "That's that motherfucker who tried to kill me!" she shouted from behind the officers.

Leo offered no resistance, nor did he utter a sound as the officers cuffed and carted him off to police headquarters at 1300 Beaubien Street in downtown Detroit. The detectives radioed the station about their arrest.

By the time they arrived, the feds, media and all respective law enforcement agencies were out front of the station, complete with flashing rooftops and an army of uniformed and plainclothes officers awaiting the killer's arrival. Most were thoroughly disappointed at the sight of the 5'5" killer, who had paralyzed two cities with his reign of terror.

Leo eventually started to talk to the more experienced detectives, offering a confession in only a roundabout way. After a 24-hour interrogation period, the detectives began to put the pieces of the puzzle in place. The one question that plagued them was the death of Nurse Darcy Owens.

Leo summed up the death of Darcy in one word, "opportunity". It took a world of self restraint for even the most seasoned detectives to not knock the block off of this smug killer.

As it turned out, Leo and Victim #6 - Porsha Freeman - had been classmates at Highland Park High School.

Leo was now an inmate in a special lockup in Wayne County Jail. Two days had passed since his arrest.

Both cities breathed a sigh of relief at the capture of the brutal killer. Psychologists from across the country all vied for a view into the mind of this elusive killer. They would all have to find another sadistic killer to study and write about, however. Leo Adams had plans for one last kill - himself.

After preparing a short letter of apology to his dead mother for not being able to save her, Leo tied a firm knot in his sheet and hung himself in his cell. A guard discovered him the next morning.

Leo took with him the details of murders that perhaps could have brought some closure to the families of the victims. The police discovered the frozen body of Mona Reed, Leo's last victim, in the basement of his home.

Detectives Jinn and Merten had been right all along: Mona was the link that connected them to the killer.

THE END

DAY WRITER PUBLICATIONS
PRESENTS

1950 Blain Street

BY AUTHOR
T. Lloyd Hardwick

1950 BLAIN STREET

Permission to reproduce in any part,
must be obtained in writing from
T. LLOYD HARDWICK
daywriterpub@gmail.com

To order call: (313) 573-2134
www.MyBookOnSale.com

MAYS PRINTING COMPANY, Inc.
15800 Livernois Avenue - Detroit, Michigan 48238
(313) 861-1900 - A Certified Minority Printer
www.MaysPrinting.com

Printed in the United States of America

ACKNOWLEDGEMENT

Special thanks to my folks, Alice Lee and Thomas Lee (Big Tommy), for giving me life - and inspiration, and my very precious wife and children, who are constant reminders of my greatest achievements.

Chapter 1

THERE IS BUT ONE WAY TO START THIS STORY.

It starts with Mama, Ava Lee Jones, a young woman, who stands about 5 feet tall, with reddish brown even-tone skin, and a figure that most men would kill for. That's exactly what her second boyfriend would do.

By now, Mama was exercising the freedom of being 18 years old, and this is how she met Sonny Hardy, a man who came from a middle class family, whose parents were good community-oriented folks, or so it seemed. His mother, Emma Hardy, was a good Christian, stand-by-your-man kind of woman, who rarely spoke out in public, except when she was praising God in church.

Sonny's father, John Hardy, on the other hand, was a well dressed, well groomed, soft-spoken man until you messed with his money. Mr. Hardy had after-hour joints east and west in the city of Detroit, and he was rumored to have hookers on the Avenue. Under the guise of a good father figure, John Hardy would take Sonny with him after school to check on his money and his women. Mr. Hardy treated the men he employed very harshly, and his women, even harder.

These same traits eventually followed Sonny into his relationships with women. One night, Mama and her friend, Rose, snuck out to an after-hour place they heard about from some friends. It just happened to be a place owned by Sonny's father. That's where Mama met Sonny. By then, Sonny was comfortable in the ways of the world and was about to inherit his father's business, whether he wanted to or not.

You see, Sonny's father had been diagnosed with cancer of the lungs and had only six months to live, and three of those were already gone before he decided to tell his family. True to the doctor's predictions, John Hardy, in fact, died of lung cancer on a cold December night and left all his business interests to his son, and most of his real estate investments to his wife, Emma.

Sonny now controlled a small empire that included after-hour joints, two very nice homes, and about 20 to 30 prostitutes active on the streets, but Sonny Hardy was nobody's pimp, not by a long shot. He had what was known as a tender dick; that's when a so-called pimp falls for the ladies he is supposed to be pimpin' after having sex with them. To make it plain, Sonny liked the ladies too much to be a pimp.

He was a big man in stature with striking dark features, like his father. He easily drew the attention of the ladies, especially my mother, who was the finest young thing at the bar that night or any other night, for that matter.

One of the barmaids instantly took a disliking for Mama and conveniently spilled a drink on her sleek-fitting brown dress that she had borrowed from Rose. Sonny had been watching Mama from across the bar all night.

"I know you ain't gonna let that bitch get away with that, Ava," said Rose.

"I sure ain't," said Mama, and just before she could smack the bitch, Sonny gently grabbed her wrist, pulled her hand to his lips, and gave her the softest kiss anyone had ever given her on any part of her body. "Since my barmaid spilled a drink on you," he said, "your drinks are on the house."

Then, he excused himself and the barmaid and they went to his office, w here he proceeded to give her a lesson in the grand tradition of his father. Tossing her to and fro, he admonished her. "Bitch, don't ever fuck with any of my customers! You got that?"

Sonny then returned to the bar, as if nothing had happened. Mama was thrilled to see him again, not realizing he had just beaten the hell out of the barmaid on her behalf.

So Mama and Sonny left the bar, leaving Rose to nurse her drinks for the rest of the night. They went to Sonny's place, and so the story goes.

A marriage, three children, and countless police reports later, Mama decided to leave, but not before Sonny literally stripped the clothes off her back and dragged her down a flight of stairs, only to throw her into the streets as naked as the day she was born. Unable to return for her children, Mama left us with Sonny. That lasted about a month, long enough for her to get a new place for the family to live.

This was 1950 Blain Street, a place that was filled with pimps, players, dealers, and the craziest people you could imagine. Nevertheless, it was all she could afford at the time. Therefore, we made do. Wherever Mama moved, Rose would follow.

Rose and Mama each had three children around the same age and size, which made for good playmates. We would play in the long, smelly hallways of the building for hours until Mama or Rose would call us in just before dark.

Mama pretty much stayed to herself, but Rose knew everyone in the building; particularly, Mr. Benny, the numbers man. Mr. Benny, by all accounts, was a one-eyed, limp-legged pervert, who liked to buy young women for sex. It was rumored that he was shot in the eye while attempting to have sex with his best friend's wife.

Mr. Benny would take the illegal numbers by phone and sometimes through the door from the few people he trusted in the building. Rose was one of the few he allowed to enter his apartment.

My brother and I ran errands for Mr. Benny all the time, but we were never allowed inside his apartment. He would take numbers from seven o'clock in the morning to six o'clock in the evening, and like clockwork, Rose was there by 6:05 p.m. and out by 7. Draw your own conclusion. Mama knew exactly what was going on, but would never speak about it. Besides, it was not the business of children, anyhow. Rose had children to support, and she did it by any means necessary.

One day there was a knock at Rose's door, and as she opened it, there stood a huge bearded man with a piercing glassy look in his eyes. He pushed his way past the chain. "Bitch, I heard you were turning tricks in the building. Is that right? Well, that shit ain't gonna happen no more, right? Right, bitch?"

As he turned to leave, he smacked Rose clean across the room and was gone as fast as he came. Rose just lay there in a frozen state. She never spoke of that night ever again, not even to my mother.

The next day, Rose searched and found a job as a cashier at a local dry cleaning establishment. While working in that capacity, the owner was training her for more responsibilities, such as pressing and cleaning clothes. While at work, Rose met a man who asked her out on several occasions, but she would always turn him down.

Then, one day, she decided to accept his invitation on the condition that she be allowed to bring a friend along. The man said, "Sure, if I can bring a friend, too."

Rose hurried home to tell Mama the news of her date and to invite Mama to go out with her. First, Mama refused Rose's offer, but with a little pressure, she gave in. She did it mostly for Rose.

Mama called Aunt Marlene to sit with us for the evening. Rose and Mama went to a small bar somewhere downtown, where they met Joe and his best friend, George, who were sitting at the bar having drinks, long before Mama and Rose arrived.

Mama was once again smitten by a man she knew little about. George was a big man with a large and intimidating presence. What attracted Mama to this man is still a mystery to me to this very day.

They started dating, and he started coming by the apartment. Soon after that, he was telling us what to do, and not six months later, he moved in.

George was a bitter and hateful man. With just a couple of drinks in his system, he was a time bomb waiting to explode, all over an undeserving woman. Then things went from bad to worse. He started beating Mama. She was always protective of her children; and so during these troubled times, she sent us to our grandfather's house so he could look after us.

Mama allowed this pattern of abuse to continue, and one month to the day after Mama sent us away, George beat her up so badly she ended up in the hospital with three broken ribs, facial lacerations, and a concussion.

That was the last straw, but certainly not the last encounter she would have with George. Mama was released from the hospital a week later and returned to her apartment on Blain Street.

Rose took it upon herself to invite a few people over to welcome Mama home. At this welcome home party, there was a man slightly taller than Mama, whom everyone seemed to know. His name was Ben, and he started conversing with Mama. As he became more interested, he asked her out, and before she could say no, he said, "Ava, once you fully recover, that is when we will go out." Mama agreed and accepted his phone number.

Ben was a hard-working man, who had married very young, had recently divorced, and was working double shifts at the auto plant, which was all he know how to do. All of this was about to change.

Ben had attended Mama's welcome home party with his best friend, Ace, a card-playing Detroit police detective, who just liked having a good time. Little did Mama know that Rose's old friend, Joe, was keeping watch on her from across the room, only later to inform George all that took place at the party.

Joe was bitter at Rose for leaving him for her longtime junky boyfriend, Rico. He was dying to exact revenge on Rose by any means necessary. Joe eventually left the party and rode down Woodward Avenue, where he just happened to run into George by the XXX Theater.

It did not take Joe very long to spill his guts to George about what happened at the party. George always intimidated Joe, and he was so pissed off at what he just learned that he grabbed Joe by the throat until he passed out.

George jumped into his Cadillac Eldorado and sped off towards Mama's apartment. He made it there in less than 10 minutes, and then pushed his way past the partygoers, only to find Mama sitting on the side of the bed, having a cigarette.

"I only want to talk to you, Ava," he said.

"You are not supposed to be here, George," Mama said. "Now, get out!

It's over between us. Don't you get it? It is over!"

"Bitch, ain't shit over till I say it's over," George countered. "Now, get yo ass over here before I break ya goddamn neck."

Mama ran over to the other side of the bed, where she grabbed a double-barrel shotgun that my grandfather had made her keep for protection. Good thing, too, as she was about to need it.

"You need to leave before..." she said to George. Before she could speak his name, she fired the first barrel straight at George's head and missed.

The 220-pound bully jumped clean through the ground floor window, only to land on his feet. He was not alone. On his trail were the blazing hot buck shots from the other barrel of the shotgun. Mama had had enough.

"There will be no more beatings here, mister!" she shouted.

From that day forward, Mama stayed strapped with a Saturday night special or a .38 caliber handgun, to be technical. She had an extra sense of confidence that said she just was not buyin' it anymore.

Ben had left the party just before all this took place, and that was a good thing, too, because Mama had no plans of telling him anything about this particular night.

Chapter 2

As for the rest of the world, it was the 70s, a time of change and hardship for black folks. Major events were taking place all around us, for which we had no concern; we were just trying to survive the neighborhood.

You see, each neighborhood was like a country unto itself. It had its trade agreements (drugs and numbers), its wars (gangs and dealers), and its politics.

None affected the neighborhood more than the series of rapes that plagued the entire west side for more than two years. The victims were young, old, crippled, blind, and crazy; if you were a female, you were at risk of being raped. It did not seem to matter to this person; he was an animal. It was rumored that he even raped a transsexual, who managed to get away with a few scrapes and bruises.

This perpetrator was a very violent person. He would beat his victims within an inch of their lives before he would sexually assault them. That's why the newspapers dubbed him the "Deadbeat Rapist".

He struck our neighborhood twice in one month without being detected. Little did we know how close to home these events would affect our family. Now, my other had three children, not counting the child she miscarried, which she affectionately called Isaac. The baby, Mama said, God wanted for himself.

Then, there was my older brother, Terrance, or Terry for short, who by all accounts was a gifted and brilliant young man. He was promoted twice while in grade school and was a member of the Honor Society. His teachers loved him. He was as naturally cunning as he was smart. Though he kept up a good front for his teachers; he gave us pure hell at home.

What we discovered in the sink were two kittens that he had drowned. My sister immediately started screaming and shouting frantically for my mother, to no avail. Mama and Rose had gone to the local market together.

I was scared, too, but more confused at the fact that Terry was busting his guts laughing at our reaction to the death of these poor little kittens. By the time Mama returned home, my sister had stopped crying, but was still visibly shaken.

Mama immediately called for Terry, but before he could answer, I spilled my guts, leaving out no details, including the clean up and disposal of those poor little kittens. As for my sister, she was not used to this level of brutality. She was a bookworm, for heaven's sake, and a bright girl in her own right. She, too, was on the Honor Roll and had a perfect attendance record.

Mama had plenty to be proud of in her children. As for me, Thomas, the baby of the bunch, I did more daydreaming in school than the law allowed. I was a less than average student with a lot of potential. When I would come home with my less-than-perfect report card, Mama would say, "You'll do better next time, son. You just have to study more."

There were not enough hours in a day to keep me satisfied. I was always the last one to go to sleep, and the first one to wake up. I had more energy than I knew what to do with.

Although our summer vacation was over, I was looking forward to September, not to go back to school, but because it was almost my birthday. Oh, what a wonderful time of year, but this birthday would be one that I would never forget. I was about to find out that the man I thought was my father (Sonny Hardy) was not my father at all.

Mama had had a brief affair with a man, whose name was - yep, you guessed it - Thomas Wilson, shortly after she left Sonny. Thomas was a professional drummer and a singer who did a lot of session work; you know that's when you go into a music studio and play background music for famous groups and get no real credit.

I later found out that he led his own little group back in the old days. I also found out that he was pretty good at his craft.

The news of this new person was a bit confusing. I did not mind the fact that Sonny was not my father; hell, he was never around anyway. The thing for me was finding out who my real father was. It became my daily obsession, and that's when I began to get into trouble in school. I was out of control. This pattern of behavior continued for several months.

Then something happened that I would never forget. It was my eighth birthday, and I was sitting at the table with a very bad attitude, and a fancy pineapple and coconut cake; where it came from, I had no idea.

Suddenly there was a knock at the door, and there on the other side of the screen stood an older woman about five feet ten inches tall with gray hair, high cheekbones, and a very large nose. Her face looked vaguely familiar.

Standing next to her was a stranger; yet it felt as if we knew one another. "Don't you recognize your grandmother when you see her?" she asked.

Before I could say a word, the strange man picked me up in the air and gave me a very hardy hug and said, "It's me, son; your old man."

At that moment, I nearly peed in my pants trying to break free from him.

"Oh, just let him go," said my grandmother. "He'll come around."

That is when I ran as fast as I could to my room and closed the door. My mother was right on my trail. "Son, how could you behave this way?" she asked. "I thought this was what you wanted! That man is your father. The same blood that runs through your veins runs through his veins as well. Give him a chance to prove himself."

And with a smile, she said, "Don't worry; I got your back, son." At that very moment, it seemed that all my fears disappeared and everything would be all right.

Chapter 3

Mama always had a way of soothing her children in their time of trouble. It would take a lot more than a hug and a few kind words to remedy what was about to happen in our lives next.

It was a cool, breezy autumn day. I had just finished my homework by the window, where I would often enjoy the refreshing cool autumn air.

My sister had completed her homework in class, as she often did. She was just about to finish her household chores, when she suddenly remembered that Wednesday was the day she would help the little old lady who lived on the second floor, doing her laundry and cleaning up her apartment. Angel started this work to keep money in her pocket for the latest fashion magazines.

Once when Angel and the old woman were doing laundry, they ran short of coins. The old woman sent Angel back to her apartment for more coins. When Angel got on the elevator, it made a sudden stop in the main lobby. A strange man got in. Angel wasn't worried; she felt right at home in the building.

Before she knew it, the man knocked her unconscious, and they were headed for the roof of the building. That was when the elevator got stuck between the seventh and eighth floors. The guy did not care; he proceeded to rape and beat my sister.

Men had been working on the roof for days. As it so happened, one of

11

the men went on his break and left the roof; that's when he found that the elevator was not working. He had to walk down a flight of stairs to catch it on the eighth floor. There, he discovered a strange man raping a young girl on the elevator. He started banging on the glass, trying to pry open the doors, to no avail.

At that very moment, the elevator started moving towards the lower floors. The roof worker took off, running down the stairs as fast as he could, only to come out on the main floor. The elevator, however, went straight to the basement, where the rapist made good his escape through the trash dock.

The family was devastated. Mama's friend, Ben, had gotten word to his detective friend, Ace, who stopped by the apartment that evening. Although rape was not his department, he promised the family he would do all that was in his power to catch the man.

Angel stayed in the hospital for nearly a week. She had suffered a brain concussion and a broken jaw. These were serious injuries for a young girl or anyone else, for that matter. My mother never left her side.

My brother and I stayed at Rose's apartment until Mama and Angel returned home. I had never seen Mama that upset before. I even heard her blame herself for what had happened. Through it all, she remained strong for her children and assured us that we would all make it through the pain.

Back at police headquarters, Ace and his detective friend, Butch Davis, were interviewing a transsexual who had called in a tip. Detective Davis - Butch, as he was known around the station - asked him to come to the station and give a description of the man who assaulted him but managed to get away. He only called the police after reading the newspaper account of Angel's assault.

Butch asked the transsexual why he had not come forward sooner. "I did not think anyone would take me seriously," he said, "so I just kept my mouth shut, except for when I did my business. Catch my drift?"

"I wonder why," the detective thought to himself.

"That will be all, ma'am," said Butch. "We will contact you if we need you."

Butch then went over to the vice department, where Ace was on the phone following up leads to the same case. Ace hung up the phone as Butch asked, "Is this about my case?"

"For sure, man," Ace confirmed. "Now, let's roll."

"Ace, you keep this up and you're going to put me out of business," Butch said. They both shared a hearty laugh and left the station.

They drove down Woodward Avenue and turned onto the 1500 block of Calvert, where they pulled in front of a large brown brick home with an old van pushed all the way back to the driveway near the back gate. Just to the left of the van were two very large barking dogs in a gated kennel.

Ace knocked on the door while Butch peeked through the curtain on the window. Much to his surprise, a fine, brown-skinned woman came toward the door. She asked through the door, "Who is it?"

"Police, ma'am," Ace replied. "We're investigating a crime that took place in this area. May we come in? We'd like to ask you a few questions, if you don't mind."

He paused for a moment or two. "Please, ma'am. It will take only a minute of your time."

"Oh, all right; give me a chance to change," she said.

She came back immediately and opened the door.

"This won't take long. I'm Detective Ace Jones and this is my partner, Detective Butch Davis. As I stated, we're investigating crimes that have been committed in this area."

"Exactly what does that have to do with me?" she queried.

"Well, ma'am, we understand from your co-worker, Madge, that you were assaulted on the third of this month. Is that true?" Ace asked.

"That bitch! She's not my friend, either. She is just someone I work with. I was not assaulted; nothing happened, thank God"

"Well, tell us what did happen and, ma'am, please don't leave out anything. Every little detail is critical to this case. Let us determine what is important or not. Now, please go right ahead," Ace said.

"If you insist...I was leaving the coffee shop after my shift ended. It was breezy but not too cool, so I decided to walk home; hell, it's only six blocks away. That turned out to be the worst decision I made in a long time. This guy came out of nowhere and he was swinging, as if he was trying to knock me out."

The two detectives looked at each other at the exact same time.

"I was wearing my white nursing shoes that night," the woman continued. "I remember clear as day while I was in the process of trying to avoid one of his punches one of my shoes came off. That was when I kicked the other one off and ran my ass off and never looked back. I will never forget this guy; he was a short, thick, smelly black dude with crazy eyes. One of them looked lighter than the other."

Butch interrupted, ""Ma'am, correct me if I'm wrong; didn't you say you were leaving the night shift?"

"That's correct," she said.

"Ma'am, how were you able to see the color of his eyes then?" Butch asked.

"Mister, I know what I saw under that damn light post," she snapped.

"You were under a light post?" Ace asked.

"Have you been listening to anything I have said? By the way, he also had a horseshoe-shaped scar over his right eye, and he smelled of mechanic's oil. I oughta know; my ex was a mechanic for 20 years. Oh, shoot," she said with excitement, "look at the time. Will that be it, fellas? I have got to get to work. I'm covering Madge's shift, believe it or not."

"We'll be in contact with you again, ma'am, if we need any more information," Butch concluded.

The detectives left the woman's house with their first solid lead. Detective Davis remembered his interview with the transsexual and how he was deliberately misleading and acting very playful. Neither behavior is the cause of an arrest, but either certainly was enough to merit a second interview.

Detectives Butch and Ace drove to the Cass Corridor, where the gay community occupied that particular section of town. They drove right up to the transsexual. He was sitting at a card table in front of the building in a pink and white robe with fluffy slippers and head full of rollers.

Ace spoke first. "We need to talk."

The transsexual hollered, "About what? I told you all that I know, baby. There is nothing more to tell."

"I think there is more to tell," said Detective Butch. "Get in the car."

Chapter 4

Meanwhile, back at the station in the interrogation room, the detectives turned up the heat on the transsexual during the interview. He eventually broke down and gave them a name, a name that the police only considered a "person of interest." However, it would be months before they would catch up with the so-called person on interest.

By now the family was adjusting to a somewhat normal life, after my sister's incident. Three great things were about to happen in Mama's life. She had recently agreed to see Ben on a regular basis; I guess his standing by the family in our time of trouble kind of appealed to her good side.

We were certainly glad to have him around the family. He was just a genuinely kind person.

Oh, yeah, another great thing was Mama's landing a job in the house-keeping department of a major hotel in downtown Detroit. Ben took us all out to a fancy restaurant to celebrate.

Despite her past trouble with men, when Mama dressed up, watch out! She was still the finest black woman on the planet or in the universe, for that matter.

By the time we finished our meal and were waiting for our dessert, Ben sat there with a serious look on his face. He grabbed Mama's hand.

"What is it," Ben," Mama asked.

"Ava, I know we have not known one another for very long, but I feel as if we have something very special, and I want to preserve it for the rest of our lives. Will you marry me?"

Mama let out a mild scream, and then she excused herself from the table. She went to the ladies room, where she proceeded to cry in the stall. That's when Ben got up and went after her. Then Angel went right behind him. She convinced Ben to let her talk to Mama first. Angel went into the ladies room only to find Mama crying her eyes out.

"Why are you crying, Mama? Ben is a pretty good person to know; besides, we like him, unlike that crazy man, George. When Ben is around, you seem to be at peace. You always taught us that peace is worth more than gold."

"Child, you have always been ahead of your time," Mama said, wiping her eyes. "Now give Mama a hug, and let's go tell Ben the good news."

Ben had been waiting at the restroom door. "Hey, Ava," he said.

"Yes, Ben, I will marry you," she said.

Ben picked up Mama and began hugging her as he twirled her in circles. They were so excited at the news; they nearly forgot that Terry and I were still at the table having dessert. I was wearing mine, after having had it smashed in my face by my big brother, who always got a kick out of torturing Angel and me.

Nevertheless, it was a good evening and everyone was happy. This happiness would be short lived; the unexpected was about to occur, and the family would never be the same.

Rose's junky boyfriend, Rico, had been cozying up to her for weeks, trying to pick her for information about Ben; asking questions, like where did he work and where did he hang out, things of that sort. Rose was in love, for heaven's sake; she did not give his questions a second thought. This information would prove to be fatal.

Rico was a scrawny dark black sneaky motherfucker who just happened to be George's number one heroin customer and would do anything to get his next fix. With the information (unwittingly) provided by Rose, George and Rico started following Ben day and night, observing his every move, waiting for the right opportunity to steal his life.

That dreadful day would come in the month of October. I remember that day as if it were yesterday. I wrote it on a calendar that I kept until I was grown up. It was an eerie night, I remember that well.

Mama and Ben had planned to marry in January and, as Ben often said, they were going to start the year off right. Unaware of how short a time he had left on this earth, Ben wanted to assure my mother that if anything happened to him, she and her children would be provided for. He told her that she was the sole beneficiary on his life insurance policy.

Mama was not trying to hear all that; she just wanted to live the rest of her life in peace with Ben and her children. Mama asked Ben to stop at the store after work to get a single can of tomato paste for the spaghetti dinner she was cooking.

On Ben's way out of the store, two strange looking men posing as crooks approached him. "Give me your wallet, nigga!" George snarled. Ben reached for his walled and at that very moment, George and Rico both shot Ben point blank in the face. He was dead before he hit the ground; he never stood a chance. Such a tragedy for such a good man! Mama was so messed up she could not attend the funeral.

Once again the family was rocked by tragedy. These were very, very dark days for us. Mama had had enough of 1950 Blain Street. She vowed that this cursed place would not claim another one of her loved ones.

We moved almost immediately to live with my grandfather for a month until Mama found us a house on Edison Street, 1420 Edison, to be exact. That is where we were to begin our new lives. The previous owner wanted to only rent the house to us; but he obviously had a change of heart. All of a sudden, we were the proud owners of a huge, five-bedroom, two-and-a-half bath beautiful brick home. It felt as though we were living in a mansion. Mama used some of the insurance money as a down payment.

Despite the few tips that came in concerning Ben's death, none of which panned out, the case went cold in a month. Ace spent much of his personal time and resources trying to solve his friend's murder, with very little results.

Just as he was about to back off the case, however, he received an anonymous phone call stating that there would be a heist in the diamond district downtown the next day. Following up on the tip, the next day Ace and a special police squad staked out the most targeted jewelry store in the area.

At that very moment, the Diamond Emporium was being robbed two blocks away. The perpetrators were none other than George and his junky friend, Rico. They ran into the place, guns blazing. As the clerk went for the alarm, Rico shot him where he stood. They were in and out in a matter of minutes.

By the time Ace and his squad responded to the call, Rico, George, and the diamonds were long gone. On the way back to the rendezvous point, George decided he no longer needed a partner. Rico never saw it coming. George gave him two bullets in the head and did not even break a sweat. He just kept on driving straight up Jefferson to Belle Isle where he dumped the car and the body, and walked back over the bridge as if nothing had happened.

Back at the crime scene, while gathering evidence, Ace asked the surviving clerk for the surveillance tape. That is when he received a call over his police-issued radio, requesting his presence on Belle Isle ASAP.

Chapter 5

Ace arrived on Belle Isle only to observe crime scene investigators examining the victim's head wounds. One investigator stated that it was a high probability that a .357 Magnum was used in the shooting. This immediately shifted Ace's mind into full gear. He remembered that the gun used to murder his friend, Ben, was a .357 Mag. "Get this guy over to the medical examiner's office ASAP," he said. "In fact, take the whole damn car in and do not touch a thing until I get there!"

Ace arrived at police headquarters, where investigators were preparing to go over the car with a fine-toothed comb. "Shall we proceed, gentlemen?" asked Ace.

Investigators dusted the car for prints and searched for bullet fragments or any trace of evidence they could find. That's when they discovered a bullet lodges in the passenger's side door. Investigators removed the bullet and rushed it over to the lab where forensic experts would later confirm a match of the bullet that killed Ben.

Now, all that was left to do was to find who killed the man in the car, the man who was given the name John Doe by the medical examiners. The police often worked with the media when they wanted to flush out criminal, so they leaked small details of the case to the local news stations, which broadcast a description of the John Doe found in the car on Belle Isle.

Rose had not heard Rico for a couple of days prior to the incident. So, when she saw the news, she thought the description hauntingly resembled that of her boyfriend. She immediately rushed down to the medical examiner's office to be sure.

The medical examiner's office was instructed by the police to call the station if anyone inquired about the John Doe found on the island. Ace was about to get a break in his case.

Rose took a taxi to the office and asked to see the John Doe she suspected was her boyfriend, Rico. That's when the medical examiner called Ace at the station and told him a lady stopped by to check on John Doe.

"I'll be right over," said Ace. "Stall her."

Meanwhile, Rose was taken downstairs, where she made a positive identification of the body. She was sitting in the lobby crying when Ace walked in.

"Ma'am, I am Detective Jones," he said. "I understand you positively identified the victim."

Rose hesitated and took a deep breath. "His name was Rico."

"Did Rico have a last name, ma'am?" Ace asked.

"Of course, he had a last name, damn it!" Rose snapped.

"Relax, ma'am. I'm here to help. Can I get you something to drink - water, coffee - perhaps a cigarette?

"I'll have a cigarette. Thank you. His name was Rico Simmons, and he knew lots of people. The man got around, you see, and he was nobody's saint, but he was all that I had." She started to cry again.

"Wait a minute," said Rose, as she seemed to snap out of her state of mourning long enough to remember the name George. "Rico would go on and on about some guy named George."

Rose had no idea that Rico's friend, George, was the same George from the past relationship of her friend, Alice.

"You wouldn't happen to know where George resides, would you?" asked Ace.

"No, sir, I don't, but Rico said George had a couple of girls on Woodward Avenue. I think that is why Rico was so fascinated with him."

"That will be all, ma'am," said Ace. "Where can we reach you if we need to?"

"You can reach me at 1950 Blain Street, Apartment 509, Detective Ace."

"Hey, I once knew a family that lived in the building," said Ace. "Never mind that; we'll be in touch."

Rose agreed to let the detective drive her home. Once there, she slid into a deep state of depression and began a drinking binge that would last for several months.

Meanwhile, Ace was slowly connecting the pieces to a very large puzzle of many colorful pieces. That's when he called his friend, Detective Butch Davis, to help sort out the details. Butch suggested that they pay the transsexual, Ms. Cleo, another visit, so that was exactly what they did.

As usual, Ms. Cleo was in his favorite daytime spot, playing bid whiz in front of his building in the Cass corridor. Butch and Ace pulled alongside Ms. Cleo.

"If somebody wanted to take you out, you wouldn't be hard to find," said Butch.

"Now, who would want to take out such a beautiful young thang like myself," said Ms. Cleo. "I'm too pretty for all that violence."

"Anyway, does the name George ring a bell?" Butch asked.

"Black George? Ring a bell? He's the most vicious pimp on the streets. He was the first player I met when I came to Detroit, but of course you knew that. Lately, he hasn't been on the set and his hoes have been out of control," Ms. Cleo offered. "One more thing: he keeps an apartment on West Grand Boulevard. I think he's in the Olde Grand Building. Yeah, that's the one."

The detectives sped off towards West Grand Boulevard without even as much as a thank you. It was time to take this guy down. They secured a warrant and assembled a tactical unit to assist in serving this high-risk warrant. The detectives arrived and were ready to enter the Olde Grand Apartments near mid-town Detroit.

The tactical unit kicked the door to George's apartment clear off the frame and proceeded to do what they do best; serve a high-risk warrant. Detectives Butch and Ace entered the apartment behind the unit.

"This guy lives like a king," said Butch, surveying the apartment with his weapon fully drawn.

"Yeah, it's nice, but let's not forget why we're here," replied Ace.

The tactical command leader made a discovery in George's bedroom closet: a beautiful young red-boned female, crouched down in the corner of the very large walk-in closet. The first words out of her mouth were, "Is this about the jewelry heist?"

Ace and Butch looked at each other in utter amazement. "Ma'am, tell us what you know about a heist," said Ace.

"I only overheard George say he would have to money to start his club after he pulled a jewelry heist," said the young girl. "That's it, I swear."

George would travel to other cities to pick up young girls, string them out on drugs, and start them on the downward spiral of prostitution. He was saving this young girl for the new strip club he was planning to open with the money from the jewelry store robbery.

Chapter 6

George had more pressing business to attend to. The young girl gave the detectives just what they needed to pick him up for questioning in the robbery and murder of the Diamond Emporium clerk. George was now a fugitive of the law. Ordinarily, he would have left the city in a heartbeat, but there was one thing left for him to do. He still had to unload the jewelry before he could blow town. He just needed a place to lay low until he got rid of the goods.

His friend, Jimmie, came to mind. He was a 6'5" beast of a man, who owned and operated an after-hour joint over the party store on the corner of Mack near Bewick Street on the city's east side. It was a place where you wouldn't want to be caught dead after dark. If there was a pit of hell, I'm sure it was in the likeness of Mack and Bewick.

You couldn't just walk in off the streets into Jimmie's place. No, siree; this place was the premier spot of the underworld, though it was not in the best of neighborhoods.

Jimmie played host to the top-notch players in the city and would not accept anything less. On any given night, you could find pimps, preachers, and politicians at Jimmie's spot. If you were somebody in Detroit, chances were you'd have stopped by Jimmie's after-hour joint. The place was very red and very plush, right down to the red-covered toilets with solid gold handles.

You had to enter Jimmie's place from the rear of the building and go up a long, specially designed staircase. However, all of this was about to come to an end.

The police received an anonymous tip; the person who made the call stated that George was hiding out above a party store on Mack near Bewick. The police knew all-too-well of the after-hours joint.

Once again, Detectives Ace and Butch and the tactical unit readied themselves to serve the warrant for the arrest of one George Ellis. Only this time, some of the officers would not make it out alive. This would turn out to be the deadliest gun battle in the history of the Detroit Police Department. Policies and procedures would be forever changed after this tragic day.

It had been extremely cold; although cold, the sky remained cloudless well into the evening hours. That's when the tactical team made its way up the fancy staircase of the two-story building. Detective Ace brought up the rear of the team, while Detective Butch was more action-oriented; he was the fifth man to enter the apartment, unaware of the dangers that awaited them on the other side of the door.

The team kicked in the door and entered the dark and quiet room. It was like a nightmare for those officers; the next light they saw was from the tip of an AK-47 with the two banana clips taped together.

Jimmie cut the officers down like they were blades of spring grass. They never knew what hit them. He then repositioned himself behind his custom-designed metal bar with the marble surface, where he had stashed two extra fully loaded assault weapons and enough ammo to battle into the next day.

Suddenly the place fell silent and, as if the assault weapons weren't enough, Jimmie pulled the pin on the hand grenade he stashed behind the bar. He rolled it across the floor towards the officers. The blast killed three officers instantly.

This soft-spoken, oversized man was on a mission to avenge the death of his younger brother, who had been killed by the police in a botched-up gas station robbery. In Jimmie's mind, he was a man with nothing to lose. There was no turning back now.

On the other hand, George had everything to gain. He still had the jewelry on his person. In all of the action, it seemed as though he disappeared, but few would be left alive to tell the story after Jimmie's grand finale. The big man stood up from his crouched position behind the bar with his arms stretched wide, shouting "I'm going to take us all to hell!"

That's when he pulled the pins on the remaining two hand grenades and blew the entire second level to pieces. The story made the national news the next day. George always said he'd be famous one day. In all, eight Detroit police officers were killed in what the newspapers called the "Motown Massacre". Among the officers killed was Detective Butch Davis.

It was one month to the day when the surviving officers attended the ceremony to receive citations for bravery in the line of duty. It was a bittersweet moment for all who attended.

Ace quietly left the ceremony after receiving his citation. There was something about the case that continued to bother him. Although emotions ran rampant at the station, Ace remained in detective mode. I guess that is what made him such an asset to the force. Besides, he had just lost his good friend of 20 years and was not going to let his death be in vain. He took a short leave of absence from work to follow a gut feeling that just wouldn't let him sleep at night.

In his pursuit of the facts, Ace would later link Ms. Cleo to George's friend, Jimmie. Evidence would further reveal that Jimmie and Ms. Cleo were related. Ms. Cleo wanted revenge just as much as his brother, Jimmie, did for the death of their younger brother. Ms. Cleo was willing to do anything to achieve this goal, even if it meant sacrificing the life of his brother.

Chapter 7

It was Ms. Cleo who tipped off the cops to George hiding out at Jimmie's. Ms. Cleo went by two days earlier to borrow money from her brother, and that's how he discovered George in hiding there. Ms. Cleo knew that Jimmie had planned to have it out with the cops one day, so he took full advantage of that fact.

Ace was not pleased; he felt he had been outwitted by a faggot transsexual that caused the death of his good friend, Butch, and several other police officers. So, it was with this new evidence that Ace went back to work and secured a warrant for the arrest of one Cleophus J. Brown, aka Ms. Cleo.

Ace arrived at the suspect's Cass Corridor apartment armed to the teeth. According to new police department policies, officers executed warrants with M16s and .45 caliber automatics as side arms.

They weren't taking any chances this time. The door was ajar when the team arrived. The officers pushed the door open and sent the police dog ahead of them waiting for his bark as a signal. The K-9 searched every room without making a sound until the dog reached the bathroom at the end of a long hallway. He began to bark frantically, as the officers advanced towards the sound of their K-9 assistant.

That's when they discovered the body of Ms. Cleo, dead in the bathtub from what appeared to be a self-inflicted gunshot wound to the right temporal region of her head.

There was no one left to interview. The suspects from Ben's case and from the Diamond Emporium heist/murder case were all dead.

Detective Ace Jones was promoted to lieutenant of his own homicide unit, and received numerous citations and accommodations for his work on those cases.

But there was still one more case that needed to be solved. That was the case of the "Dead Beat Rapes" of which my sister was a victim.

Chapter 8

By then, the family had settle down and was living peacefully in our new home on Edison Street in what is now known as the historic Boston-Edison District, where there are considerably large, beautiful, well-kept homes.

On our block, there were only three or four families with young children; other than that, the block largely consisted of old folks who maintained their properties with the precision of professionals. Not as much as a blade of grass stood out of place on this block. I wish I could say the same for the family that lived directly across from our house.

The characters that lived there were as colorful as a rainbow. The Jacob family had the most unique house on the block or in the entire area, for that matter. Their beautiful two-story home had four bedrooms and two-and-a-half baths; outside, there were large protruding stones down the front lawn with a winding walkway that led you to the arched entrance of their home.

I was impressed even as a boy at the design of this house, whose owner was none other than Mr. Jacob, a tall, slender, good-looking man, with dark, wavy hair and a deep, raspy voice.

Mr. Jacob was a hardworking auto plant foreman for one of the Big Three auto makers in Detroit. He lived with his wife, who was a stay-at-home wife. Well, let me rephrase that for you; Mrs. Jacob didn't work for a living, and she didn't stay at home, either. She was a fancy woman, a woman of leisure, one who was always traveling from place to place.

She went to Las Vegas at least three times a year, which suited Mr. Jacob just fine. He had maintained a long-time affair with a woman named Janice, who lived on Taylor Street, and he wasn't about to give her up any time soon.

Although his wife was a true fox in her own right, Mr. Jacob had tasted the honey from another hive and loved it. He would buy new Cadillacs every few years for him and his wife. The entire neighborhood, including myself, thought the Jacob family was rich.

As you can imagine, with their father always at work and their mother always gone somewhere, the children were left to their own devices. First, there was the oldest son, Larry, who was a very flamboyant person. It was believed that he was gay before it was popular to be so. "Larry Love" as his friends in the gay community called him, was a very talented singer with a short fuse. He divided his time between Detroit and California, where some would say club owners would hire him for his singing, but fire him for his attitude. Once again, Larry Love was on his way to California for an audition at the expense of his parents.

There were other colorful members of the family besides Larry. There was Dina, the middle child, a young girl who spent way too much time talking about boys and clothes. Every guy in the area wanted to date Dina. I am not kidding; the girl was fine. Most of the guy trying would get their chance; Dina was as loose as a goose on an oil slick.

Last but certainly not least was Damon, the kid who was definitely a contender for the devil's throne. They called him "Damon the Demon", a name given to him by some of the older folks in the neighborhood. He took the business of mischief to another level. He blew things up, vandalized private property, and stole things he had absolutely no use for.

Now, imagine Damon and my brother, Terry, together. Well, hold onto your book. These two devilish creatures were like two peas in a pod. They complemented each other in every way. They began their reign of terror just one block over from our house by painting a neighbor's dog from nose to tail with bright lavender house paint left over from my sister's room.

If that wasn't enough, they taped a series of firecrackers around the dog's neck and lit the fuses. The dog lost hearing in both ears and its owner eventually had to put their beloved German Shepherd down. This little stunt would cost my brother a six-month stay in a juvenile home for boys, where he further perfected the craft of lies and deception.

Once again, the Jacobs bailed their son, Damon, out of another mess. He never served a day of time. This pattern of rescue only enforced Damon's sense of "no matter what he did, there were no consequences for his actions." In Damon's mind, there was no incentive to do good. This would later lead to his demise.

For me, the little bow-legged kid that daydreamed way too much, these were pretty good days. I made a few friends in the neighborhood and pretty much stayed out of trouble. Well, there was this one time when I was visiting my friend Ricky at the end of the block. His older brother had a few of his friends over for what they called a "freak-out". Please allow me to explain. A freak-out is when a bunch of guys gets together to drink, talk shit, and have sex with one or more willing females. Some call it "running a train"; I call it downright nasty, but who am I to say?

T. LLOYD HARDWICK

Chapter 9

I was just a kid on my way to the bathroom to relieve myself and before I knew it, Ricky's big brother pulled me dead into the center of the action. I was scared to death. The room smelled of sex, funk, and alcohol, but nothing could have prepared me for what was to happen next. Ricky's brother asked me, a kid of a tender age, if I had ever seen a pussy before. I began to shake like a leaf.

Meanwhile, half of his crew continued to have sex with the young girl, while the other half was busy taunting and cracking their sides in laughter at my reaction to the brother's question. If that wasn't enough, one of the guys said, "You're up next, kid" and he pushed me right between a pair of long, silky smooth legs that stretched from one end of the room to the other, or so it seemed. As it turned out, the girl lying on the floor was my neighbor, Dina Jacob, who received me with no resistance.

Dina had her hands all over me as if she wanted me next. That's when I pissed all over myself in fear. I was kicking and screaming as loud as I could, and then I finally broke away from her and ran through a gang of laughter and ridicule. So what? I was free. I ran as fast as I could through the alley to our house in the middle of the block. It felt like it was a mile away, but I finally reached the back door and ran up the back stairs to my bedroom.

I sat for hours, too embarrassed to tell anyone what had just taken place. I have never spoken of that incident until now. I never went on the inside of any of my friends' homes again.

I was far from being a saint, and I did my fair share of mischief, as well. Let's see; there was the time when I was waiting on our porch to be picked up by my grandmother for a weekend visit, while Terry and Damon were planning their next assault on whatever they could get their hands on.

When my grandmother arrived, Terry decided he would ask her if Damon could stay over for just one night. She agreed. That would turn out to be the worst decision she would ever make.

We placed our stuff in Peaches' very large Cadillac Sedan Deville. Yes, I called my grandmother Peaches. She went by no other name; even her pastor called her Peaches. She was a very sassy, church-going, cake-bakin', fancy-dressin', no-nonsense kind of woman, who was about to get the surprise of her life.

Peaches lived in a beautiful area of Detroit known as LaSalle Boulevard. Her home was without a doubt the biggest and best kept in the area. She had just had her kitchen remodeled to accommodate her baking business.

We had just finished our lunch in the little cozy breakfast nook just off the back of the kitchen. We were about to watch television in the den, when my grandmother informed us that she had some errands to run and would return in a short while.

That short while turned out to be four long hours, long enough for us to completely trash her beautiful home. It looked like a tornado had hit the inside of her home. Her beautiful French provincial furniture was overturned but not before receiving our names in whipped cream.

We had a food fight right in the middle of her very elegant dining room. We broke everything from china to the chandelier. Most of the things in the china cabinet could not be replaced, because they were things that had been handed down through her parents and grandparents, which made those items priceless.

We made a total mess of the place and didn't bother to stick around to find out what my grandmother's reactions would be to her new décor.

We later discovered that when she walked into her house, she screamed at the top of her voice and ran to the neighbors to call the police. She thought that real criminals had broken in and vandalized her home. I can only imagine the shock to a person who kept her home in such immaculate condition. She vowed that no kids would ever set foot in her house again, family or otherwise.

Peaches phoned me a year later to wish me a happy birthday. And, as sure as the sun rises in the east, I would never again see the inside of her house.

My father continued to come around. Although what we did was wrong, he got a good laugh out of it all. He always did think that his mother was too attached to material things.

My father and I had a unique relationship. I didn't miss him all that much when he was away, but when he did come by, everybody was happy. He treated my brother and sister as if they were his own children. We had tons of fun and made lots of good memories.

Dad was one of those genuinely kind-spirited people you meet once in a lifetime, if you're lucky. I guess that made me the luckiest kid in the world. Although I was hurt when he passed away, I didn't feel the least bit cheated. Yes, this sweet, kind soul of a man drank himself to death. I still miss him to this day. I know that his spirit of kindness dwells in me daily.

Chapter 10

Meanwhile, in other parts of the city, the Dead Beat Rapist took his act to the east side of Detroit. The people of Detroit had just elected its first black mayor, and he wasn't having it. His first order of business was to form a multi-unit task force geared toward solving these rape cases with Detective Ace Jones as lead detective.

The mayor grew up on Detroit's east side, so the case became top priority to law enforcement officers. Detective Ace went back over all of his old notes with task force officers. That's when one of the officers noticed missing pages from Detective Butch Davis' notepad. As you recall, Detective Davis was killed in the line of duty in one of the worst shootouts in Detroit police history. So Detective Ace went through a box of his old friend's effects that he had kept in his locker.

It was just about time for Detective Ace to leave work one day. He took the box home with him with him, and in a rush to answer his telephone after arriving home, he positioned the box only halfway on the table. As he reached to secure the box, he knocked it onto the floor. What Ace then discovered changed his life forever.

An envelope was taped to the bottom of the box on the inside with the word "finally" written on it. Upon opening the envelope, Ace was surprised to find a key to a safety deposit box at a local bank, and a note containing all the information needed to retrieve the contents thereof.

For the first time in Ace's career, he appeared to be baffled. He had a funny feeling about what was in the safety deposit box, so he placed the key and letter in the glove compartment of his unmarked police car and kept it there for the next two days.

Ace did not want to hinder progress on the case, so he finally drove to the National Bank of Detroit on the corner of Grand River and Joy Road. Nervous with anticipation, he entered the bank, presented the proper papers, and by escort went into the vault area where, upon opening the safety deposit box, he made a devastating discovery. He found a note typed on police department letterhead, which said:

"If you're reading this letter, I am no longer alive. I, Detective Butch Davis of the Detroit Police Department's Violent Crime Unit, have deliberately withheld vital information concerning the "Dead Beat" rape case. I had no knowledge of the first four or five cases until my sister called me with the news. She told me that her son, my nephew, was raping all of these women in Detroit, and she begged me not to turn him in. I didn't know what to do. Embarrassment and shame clouded my judgment as detective. Just try to imagine being in my shoes for a moment.

"I went to his job several times intending to kill him, but I just couldn't bring myself to do it. I would even follow him around to try and catch him in the act, but nothing ever happened.

"His name is Timothy Davis, and he has worked at Al's Auto Shop since he was a kid. It's over for me, and there's only one way out.

"P. S. I'm sorry!"

Ace wept as if he had lost a child. It was over; the case of the serial rapist had finally run its course.

It took nearly three years to solve these cases. A good officer had fallen, and the chief suspect that paralyzed the city with fear and anxiety was in police custody, but there was one more thing left on Ace's "to do" list.

He drove to our house on Edison Street to inform us of the arrest. Little did he know that we had watched it on the 6:00 news and were celebrating with chocolate cake and Kool-Aid, when Ace rang the doorbell.

It was a bittersweet moment for the seasoned detective, who was still the professional person that everyone had come to know. He drove my sister, Angel, and me to police headquarters, where without hesitation or doubt, Angel identified the man as her attacker.

Three other women later came forward to make positive identification, which would guarantee Timothy Davis a life sentence in Jackson State Prison.

Chapter 11

So we made it through the court dates, conviction, and sentencing, and we were ready to resume a normal life. That's when an unexpected enemy hit the family.

The winds of change were blowing dark clouds our way once again. The hotel that Mama was working for had scaled back its workforce by 50 percent, and Mama was no exception.

She was no fool, though, when it came to managing a dollar. She bargain-shopped like it was her religion, but all the bargain shopping in the world could not ward off this next set of events. Mama was about to lose our house, our dog, and all of her self-control.

She had been very careful with the remaining insurance money that her dearly departed fiancé, Ben, had left her. If you may recall, she used only a small portion of the money as a down payment on the house we lived in at the time.

Here's where the trouble began. They say that "no one can hurt you worse than family", and that's true. His name was Charlie or "Charlie the Cheater", a name my uncle wore like a badge of honor.

This brother was slicker than an oil spill on a rainy day; he could talk a hungry dog off a meat truck. The guy was good at his craft; good enough to talk Mama out of her remaining $10,000 without even breaking a sweat.

He told her he would double her money in two months with her initial investment returned in a month. As it turned out, my uncle did show up two months later, but empty handed. The Negro had the nerve to show up in a brand spanking new Cadillac Eldorado.

He never got out of the car. He just blew the horn like some crazy fool, as he stood on the seat of the all-white leather seats with the red trim; the other half of his body protruded through the sunroof like a fool. I'll never forget that day as long as I live.

Our living room sofa was propped up by a brick that Mama had brought in from the backyard. I had been sitting on the porch, minding my own business. Before I could tell Mama that Uncle Charlie was outside, she broke through the already fragile screen door with the brick in her hand.

Mama ran halfway up the long sidewalk, aimed, and launched the reddish brown brick clean through the passenger side window of my uncle's bright, shiny new Cadillac.

After he cooled off, he phoned my mother to apologize and to give her $1,000 of the money back. Imagine that. Mama accepted the money and my uncle's apology with a smile; after all, he was still her brother.

Later that night, Mama walked four blocks over to where one of Uncle Charlie's favorite ladies lived, and with a full can of gasoline, set the Caddy ablaze. The interior burned like a moth in a flame.

This small victory would be short-lived, however. My mother was arrested that night for arson, only to be bailed out by an old family friend, Detective Ace Jones. Mama explained to Ace why she had set the fire, and he used his influence to get the charges reduced to vandalism, which was the best he could do.

All hope was lost on saving our home from foreclosure. Mama was still out of work and two months behind in her mortgage payment. As you can imagine, we lost our home and had to move almost immediately.

Ace told my mother about some property a few blocks away that his mother had left to him. We were able to live there until Mama got back on her feet. She later paid Ace a monthly rental fee of $200. The address was

1255 Clairmount Avenue.

It was 1980. Disco was dead, rap was coming alive, and Ronald Reagan was president. I was, by then, what old folks referred to as "smelling my piss." I didn't get into trouble all that much, but I did catch the hustling bug. At 12 years of age, I was selling $1 joints on the corner of Hamilton and Clairmount in front of the Arab's party store.

Everybody on the block was involved in some kind of hustle, from Mrs. Lacey who sold watered down liquor to the card-hustling family that sold fireworks and homemade ice cream. There was never a dull moment on Clairmount Avenue. It was the training ground for all young, would-be hustlers.

Chapter 12

While in pursuit of higher learning at CSU, which stands for Clairmount Street University, my sister, Angel, went to live with my grandfather on the east side, where she would complete her last year of high school at Martin Luther King High School.

My brother, Terry, was about to serve his first bit of time for breaking and entering. Of all the places in the world to break into, he chose a cop's house on Chicago Boulevard. Terry stole the officer's service revolver, along with his antique gun collection.

Terry was not alone in this endeavor. He was aided by none other than his good friend, Damon Jacob, from Edison Street. They, too, were perfecting the art of criminal intentions. The only difference between them and me was that I was in it strictly for the money. For Damon and Terry, it was all about the action.

A few years went by, and I became bold in my demeanor, not disrespectful, but just cocky as hell. Y'all know how we get when we start making a little money. I had a brand new Cadillac Cimarron, and you couldn't tell me shit. I was never big on jewelry; that whole big rope era passed me right by. I was, however, heavy into my gear-Fila shoes, sweat suits, and all things Gucci-Gucci socks, shoes, and wristbands. If Gucci made it, I had it. This was accomplished primarily by selling marijuana. But all this would pale by comparison to what was about to change my life next.

I was about to enter into the dangerous high stakes world of weight cocaine; you know, brick, birds, kilos, etc. I had paid my dues in the alley-ways and on the street corners. It was time to go to the next level; one girl and her family would take me there.

In my quest for true hustler status, I would make more money than I had ever seen in my life, catch two bullets in the belly, and fall hopelessly in love with the niece of the biggest drug kingpin the city of Detroit had ever seen. Mama eventually went back to work; my brother Terry went from jail to jail; and I, Thomas Hardy, was about to meet the man himself, "Black Sam."

It was at a George Duke concert during intermission when I first met the King of Cocaine. Samuel Percy Gossette, aka Black Sam. This buy was as big as they come in the drug business. Sam was accompanied by his beautiful young niece, Nya, with whom I became smitten at first glance. This had to be the single most beautiful creature I had ever laid my eyes on, ever! They looked like an ordinary father and daughter out having a good time at a concert, except for the oversized bodyguards lurking in tow.

We were standing in line at the concession stand when Nya's million-dollar-smile caught my eye. Sam turned to me just as I was about to speak. He knew my name and where I lived. What he would say to me next would forever change my life. He told me that he had heard about me around the neighborhood and liked they way I kept my head low when it came to doing business.

What Sam asked me next caught me completely off guard. He asked me to come by his house on Boston and Second Avenue for a backyard bar-becue. My answer was an immediate "sure, no problem"; this wasn't the type of guy you said no to, especially if you wanted to go anywhere in the business. I wanted it all - lock, stock, and barrel.

By sheer determination, I had placed myself on the fast track of crimi-nal gain. There were only three places left in my world for me to go: jail, the grave, or straight to the top. I had no interest in the first two. I spent a sleepless night in awe of being invited to the house of my mentor.

The next day I pulled in front of what had to be no less than a Hollywood mansion, except that I was still in Detroit. That's when one of those thick-necked, muscle-bound brothers that accompanied Sam to the concert motioned me to drive alongside the palace to a special underground parking garage. It was mind blowing. I had never seen a place like this, except on television or in the movies.

I got out of my car only to be greeted by a sister with long gray dreadlocks and a face that said she had lived somewhat of a challenging life. The woman escorted me to an elevator that took me up one level to the pool area.

There I stood at the end of what appeared to be the largest pool in the world, at least for me. At the other end was a grand buffet loaded with barbecue ribs, steaks, lobster, and much more. I thought that I had arrived too soon, but before I could say a word, Sam swung open the French doors of his balcony, as he appeared to be in an intense conversation, looking like a black Hugh Hefner. This guy was it, y'all; the red silk robe with the black ascot around his neck. The only thing missing were a pipe and slippers.

Sam never dressed up when he was in the streets; he said it drew too much attention. He would also say, "The less they notice, the less they know." I would later govern my affairs on that same principle.

Sam gestured me with one finger, letting me know he would be down in a minute. I kept waiting for others to show up for the barbecue, but no one ever came. This meeting of ours would turn out to be more of an elevation ceremony than anything.

Sam didn't have anyone working for him directly. It was as simple as supply and demand; you would buy and Sam would supply. Sam had just sealed the deal with the Mexicans to move 1000 kilos a month, for starters. He had recently lost two of his top clients to a petty street beef over some young chick that was playing them both. One thing led to another, and two good hustlers were dead.

Though Sam had a keen eye for talent, no man can predict the behavioral pattern of another. He had made a great number of young brothers very rich. Anybody who was somebody in this business go their start with this guy, and I would be no exception. It was my turn to shine, and I was as ready as any one person could be.

We must have talked of our plans for at least five hours straight. That's when I asked to use the bathroom. On my way there, I noticed the door next to the bathroom was slightly ajar, just enough for me to get the most pleasant surprise of my young life.

There stood Sam's 5'2" beautifully even-toned, smooth-skinned niece, Nya, as naked as the day she was born. I simply froze in my tracks as I watched her apply body oil from head to toe. This was more than a sexual arousal for me. Coupled with the perfumed oil that Nya was using, which managed to find its way to my olfactory system, this turned out to be a truly angelic experience for me. As you can imagine, I never made it to the bathroom.

By the time I got back, Sam was no longer at the table. Out of nowhere appeared the woman with the gray dreadlocks. She delivered a verbal message from Sam, "Eat light and be ready." That simply meant that we would meet at a designated place and bring plenty of money.

It was on.

I immediately reduced my crew from four to two of my most trusted soldiers. Sam had told me in our meeting that the moment I did that, I would create an instant enemy. The man didn't survive the drug wars of the 60s and 70s with his life and not know what he was talking about. Low and behold! The unthinkable was about to happen.

We still had product left to move, and as a policy of mine, I would collect the money from the weekend sales on Sunday morning. There were only two cats that had this knowledge. One was Robert Foster, aka "Cold-blooded", and the other was me. Cold-Blooded was my enforcer; when the rules needed to be enforced, he was the one who got the job done.

I'll admit I had to yank his leash on a couple of occasions, but he was controllable and reliable. All of that was about to change. Cold-blooded was one of the cats I chose to go along with me on my journey to the top. This decision would prove to be bad from the start. Of course, I informed him of my plans, which obviously didn't set well with him. He began a plot to rob me of the two things I valued most: my life and my money.

Chapter 13

Cold-Blooded must have followed me much of the afternoon waiting for a chance to kill me. This cat wasn't the hard-core killer folks thought he was. However, when you put money, guns, and drugs together, you create a lethal combination, and I was about to find that out the hard way.

Before that day, I never felt the need to carry a gun on my person; I always kept it in my glove compartment. I thought I was the shit. I trained like a boxer for my own personal satisfaction. This guy didn't share the same respect that the rest of the crew had for me. He feared me, but he obviously managed to keep up a good front. Perhaps that's why he hired a skinny crack-head, bubble-eyed, dope fiend to do what he could not bring himself to do.

I was waiting in my rented Pontiac 6000 for the light to change at the corner of Clairmount and 14th Street when a silver Jeep driven by Cold-blooded drove alongside and honked the horn in broad daylight.

That's when the bullets from a .45 caliber automatic found their way into my chest and upper abdomen. By all accounts, this should have been it for me. The two cowards sped off, leaving me and $11,000 stashed in the glove compartment. Sam got word of what happened to me before I arrived at the hospital. Let's just say, I'm here and the shooters are not, so let's leave it at that.

Although I was grateful that Sam removed my little problem, I didn't feel the least bit indebted to him. He was only protecting his business interests. As it turned out, I would spend the next two weeks in Receiving Hospital. Nearly everyone I was acquainted with either stopped by or sent flowers or cards to my room. The doctors finally instructed the nurses not to allow any more flowers in my room.

All but two of the bullets were removed from my body, and my recovery went pretty fast. Sam never came to the hospital to see me; he was funny that way, but he did allow his beautiful young niece, Nya, to visit me.

I was in the bathroom looking at myself in the mirror. All of a sudden, that familiar fragrance of hers found its way to my nose. My first physical reaction was in the form of perspiration beads on my forehead. I was in no condition to receive such a visit.

Then, she spoke and that's when her soft, sweet voice filled the room with angelic harmony. "Thomas, are you in the bathroom?"

"Ya, sure, I'll be right out." I eventually pulled myself together and came out of the bathroom in my silk paisley robe with my colostomy bag attached to my side.

Even in my present condition, I managed to find these kind words, "What god have I pleased to be worthy of your majestic presence?"

"Oh, so you're a poet?" she responded.

"No, but I manage to say the right things when I'm inspired."

"That was very pretty, and I hope you are inspired more often," she said.

It felt like we were communicating in a language all our own. Nya placed a card on my bedside table and made me promise not to open it until she left.

I was so excited at our mutual exchange that I smiled and shit on myself simultaneously (in my bag, of course). My nurse just happened to drop by for blood, much to my favor.

That's when Nya gracefully made her exit, making the phone-in-hand gesture and whispering, "I'll call you tonight. Don't forget the card."

How could I forget such a beautiful card? After being changed by my nurse, I finally opened the card to a treat that could be appreciated only in the depths of reminiscence.

This thoughtful young soul had put the same perfume oil on the card that she wore the day I had the privilege of witnessing her in her natural nakedness. The card simply read: Is there room in your life for a friend?

These simple words changed my way of thinking. Before Nya, I had thoughts only of my own selfish needs, not concerning myself with the needs of others.

Over the next two years, Nya and I would become very, very close, and I would become very rich, or what is known as "nigga rich", which simply means having ridiculous amounts of cash and having no investments or plans for the future. I had no use for niggas or neighbors, so I moved.

I purchased a nice, four-bedroom ranch-style home not far from Metro Airport in Romulus, Michigan. I had grown tired of the same old faces patting me on the back, not knowing when that pat on the back would become a knife in the ribs.

Mama didn't want to move, and she would not accept any of my "street money", as she called it. Nya and I made plans to hook up in Florida, where she attended a black college tour. She had expressed an interest in Florida A & M, which was the last stop on the tour. All my business affairs were in order, and there would not be another shipment until the end of the month. I was free to go - no boss, no bother. I paid Nya's chaperone $500 to look the other way for a few hours and promised to have her back before breakfast.

We laughed, talked, played, ran, fell down, got up, and fell in love this quiet and perfect night. I didn't want the night to end. It was about four o'clock in the morning, and we weren't the least bit tired. Although I had fallen in love with Nya, lust for her body never entered my mind. I simply adored this person in every sense of the word, and I wanted our souls to be joined for all eternity. There was no other girl for me.

We stayed outside of her hotel room to watch the sun rise. We must have kissed for 10 full minutes. I would not see Nya again until we were back in Detroit, where we were allowed to date under the strict supervision of Sam and his two bodyguards. Sam was a smart man. Instead of driving his niece away, he allowed her certain freedom to learn and explore things in life. Besides, he thought I was a pretty good guy for Nya to know.

I was desperate to show Nya my house in Romulus. At that time in our relationship, the only way that would happen would be to invite Sam to join us, as well. This would later prove to be a very costly mistake.

I invited Nya, Sam, and his henchmen to my house for an afternoon of fun in the sun. Well, at least Nya and I were enjoying ourselves. We swam like two fish in a bowl in my newly installed heated pool, as Sam and his bodyguards looked on.

Sam talked on the phone much of the time he was there; that was just Sam being Sam, always doing business.

We played like children for hours. I was in my glory. I had the girl, the cash, and the favor of Detroit's only true and living kingpin. It was a dream come true.

Chapter 14

My dream was about to become a nightmare, and my whole world would come tumbling down, kilo by kilo. What would happen next would upset the entire Detroit drug market. It was now the 1990s; George W. Bush, Sr., was in office, and drugs were plentiful. The 90s produced more independent dealers in the history of the game. The day of the large crews was gone. It was all about self and selfishness. The young, independent dealers were making their mark in the game. Young guys with a shelf-life of about one or two years, tops, if they were lucky.

These guys had very little respect for themselves and even less respect for the game. They shot everything that moved and did not agree with them. They only brought more heat on themselves and their business interests.

For the first time in my life, I considered getting out of the game, so I made a promise to myself, along with my plan to get out of the biz with my cash, my girl, and my life.

Things were going pretty well for me. Nya was about to finish her junior year at Florida A & M and was excited about my flight to Florida to pick her up for summer break. I was so much in love with her. We planned to rent a car in Florida and drive back to Detroit, just so we could spend those hours together. Only this time, business would prevent me from making the trip, a decision I would regret for the rest of my life and one that

Sam would never forgive me for making.

After informing Nya of our change in plans, she decided to catch a ride with one of the girls in her dorm that lived in Flint, Michigan, a one-hour drive north of Detroit. They had driven only five hours when a double-loaded semi truck hit the little red Saturn Coupe head on and completely demolished the vehicle. Later reports showed that the vehicle was reduced to a third of its original size. They never stood a chance.

Students at the dorm said that the girl driving the car had been up for two nights partying out of control and must have fallen asleep at the wheel. I just remember my life coming to an end. Nya was my rock, and she was the air that I breathed; she was my reason for living.

To this day, I don't remember her funeral. The memory is obviously erased from my mind. The greatest part of me had just died with her.

Chapter 15

For Sam, Nya was his lifeblood. He rescued her from the neglectful hands of his heroin-addicted sister when Nya was only about two months old. Geraldine Percy had her sleeping in a dresser drawer on the floor of a rundown apartment in Highland Park.

Sam raised her to be a kind and respectful young lady. Her life was his life.

At first, after the accident, Sam was in denial. He simply could not accept the fact that his beloved niece was gone and would never come back. Denial would soon turn to anger, which Sam would direct straight towards my head.

As you could imagine, I was finished with the drug game in the city of Detroit or anywhere else on the planet. Sam made damn sure of that. The shrewd, calculating businessman that I had come to know was beginning to lose his edge. He began conducting business with those young renegade cats from the neighborhood that had only heard of the legend of Black Sam and, quite frankly, didn't give a damn about him or his name, as he would later find out.

As for me, I stuck around the house for nearly a month grieving and drowning in my sorrow. Then, out of the clear blue sky, I had a vision. It would not come to fruition until the winds of drama blew again into my life.

Of course, Sam continued to blame me for Nya's death. I was conducting business that benefited both of us, but nothing could sway his thinking. In his mind, I might as well have been driving that semi myself.

I was out of the game and trying to piece my life back together, so I sought out the one person who could make everything all right - again, Mama, a one of a kind woman. God bless her soul forever.

Mama was worried about me and my state of mind. She made me stay with her for a couple of days, and that did me a world of good. Mama had mastered the art of comforting her children in their time of need. I felt damn good about myself again.

Such was not the case for Mama. Her health was failing, and she needed to have heart surgery. After receiving a call from my sister, Angel, I rushed home to gather some of my personal items so that I could be with Mama in her time of need.

I opened the door to my home, only to find that it had been ransacked and vandalized. I walked down the hallway past the guest rooms to the master bedroom. There was nothing there that this person or persons had not smashed to a pulp. Everything was literally destroyed.

After the initial shock of seeing my place in such disarray, I moved towards the safe that I had bolted in my closet floor beneath the carpet. Needless to say, the safe was gone. I went down on one knee and nearly fainted like a bitch. My life's work was in that safe along with the ring I planned to give Nya and the first $100 I ever earned on the street. All that was left was my house.

There was not doubt in my mind who was behind this madness: Sam. I found out later that the guys who broke into my house were there to steal my life. Black Sam would never get the chance to remove me from the planet, however. His own days were swiftly coming to an end.

With the help of one of Sam's long-time bodyguards, the young guys he had been doing business with broke into his home on Boston Street with the alarm mysteriously turned off at four in the morning. They shot Sam four times in the head and cut his throat from ear to ear, and then stole half a million dollars in cold cash.

Some say Sam wanted to die after Nya's death. A man who had been so careful for so long finally met his doom. That was the legend of Black Sam.

Chapter 16

For the first time in years, I was broke. I still had the house in Romulus, but I didn't feel comfortable living there after the break-in, so I moved in with my mother in Highland Park, where I lived until I got back on my feet.

Mama's surgery was successful, and she was recovering very well. Angel also moved back home to assist Mama with her daily care.

I helped out as much as I could, but I could not ignore the hustler brewing inside my soul. Then one day, it hit me, so I took a trip over to the shopping complex on Warren and Conners, where my old buddy, Big C, had a thriving barber shop. This guy was the best in the business. He was also my main man, one hundred grand.

Big C was once a businessman in the streets also, but he was smart with his money. He paid cash for a rundown home in a good neighborhood and turned it into a palace. As for the shop, he was the only brother that owned his building.

Big C offered me a job before I could fix my mouth to ask. I started out cutting children's hair and like everything else in life I would attack the task like a pit bull on a soup bone. In less than two years, I was cutting hair for adults to the tune of 30 to 40 heads a day and growing. I achieved this by working when no else was willing to do so. This gave me a niche. I would work on Sunday and Monday, when most shops were closed. I was making a killing in the barber business!

Big C let me have the run of his place. I stacked my cash day after day and month after month until I was comfortable enough to make a move.

I sold my house in Romulus and purchased a building on Van Dyke between 7 and 8 Mile Roads. You wouldn't believe the deal I got on this place. I stripped it down and fixed it into one of three premier shops on the east side of town.

The same principles of the drug game apply in business, as well: work hard, stack your cash, and move on to the next level. Once again, I was back on the track of financial gain. Only this time, it was all legit.

The grand opening of my spacious, 12-chair barber shop, "The Critical Cuts", was very successful. The shop was beautiful, complete with two shoeshine stands and a glass block reception area.

Mama, Angel, and all of my closest friends were there to support my latest venture. Mama was just happy to see the changes I had made in my life. Even with all the good that was happening in my life, drama was still lurking in the shadows.

Some unknown person tried to burn down my shop with what fire officials said was a gasoline cocktail just one month after my grand opening. Lucky for me, the fire only scorched the windows and burned the vinyl awning, which melted like candle wax.

I closed the shop long enough - just one day - to have a roll-up door installed, and then it was business as usual. I never knew who set the fire and I didn't want to know. I just wanted to run my shop in peace, but that wasn't always the case.

For instance, it was a Sunday morning, of all days, for the drama to take place. I wasn't the most religious person in the world, but there was something about church music and Sunday mornings that went hand in hand, so I began playing church music from 9 a.m. to 12 noon. I had informed most of my regular clients before doing so.

Change never fails to bring forth a challenge. And, as for niggas, there's always one in the crowd.

Chapter 17

This guy was a new jack, new to the shop and new to the game. He had been in the shop once or twice before. You could tell he was making gym shoe money; his type was all too familiar to me. He reminded me nothing of myself, but made me feel good to be free of that lifestyle.

This guy had the big car, the big jewelry, and the big mouth, one of which I would personally close for him. The guy was off the hook, y'all!

He immediately started complaining about the church music that had been playing long before he arrived; besides, who the fuck was he to say? As if that wasn't enough, y'all, this little nigga fired up a joint in my restroom. You could smell it throughout the entire shop. This was the straw that broke the camel's back.

I promptly stopped cutting Mr. Dickson's hair to put an end to this mess. Little did I know it was only the beginning. This fool was sitting on the sink in the restroom smoking what had to be the biggest joint I had ever seen in my life.

"What the hell are you doing in here?" I asked.

"Getting high, nigga, what it look like?" he responded.

Y'all don't know what it took for me not to cold cock this young fella. Back in the day, it wouldn't have taken that much for him to get his motherfuckin' head split wide open to the white part, but I was a changed man.

63

A friendly hello and a smile was how I greeted folks, and kind words were my weapons of choice.

I firmly asked this guy to extinguish his joint and get his ass out of my restroom. I returned to my station to finish Mr. Dickson's haircut.

Not a minute later, this guy comes out of the restroom, walks through the middle of the shop, stops at my station, and says, "What the fuck are you looking at, nigga?"

My clients were in awe. They expected me to deal with this guy right away. I would not disappoint their call for blood. Before I could give it a second thought, brother man was on the floor bleeding profusely from the head. I had struck him across the forehead with the Andis-Master clippers I had been using on my client, and then I kicked him in the ass once he fell to the floor. Next, I did something I never thought I would do. I called the police, who, in turn, called the Emergency Medical Unit.

I told the police what had happened, and they responded by laughing and advising me to make a report of the matter as soon as possible. While the young guy was being treated for his injuries, the police ran his name through the squad car computer. Turns out the guy had a warrant out for his arrest.

This would not be our last encounter. Fate would bring us together again for one last showdown.

Prior to the drama, I had hired a new receptionist to answer the phone and schedule appointments. She was to start work the next Monday morning. The young woman was cute, sassy, and fresh out of college. She had not been able to find a job in her field of study.

Although Tanya Knotts was a little sassy, she had not missed a day of church since she was a child. There were two things Tanya was very sure about in her life: her relationship to God and the type of man she didn't want in her life.

She had watched her mother go from one bad relationship to another after the death of her father, a dedicated deacon at their church. Tanya made a promise to God and to herself that the man she dated had to belong to somebody's church or he wasn't for her. He had to have a relationship with God.

Tanya was a cute, shapely girl, in whom I had no personal interest whatsoever at that time. She was my employee; it was as simple as that.

The Critical Cut Barber Salon was a hit. Word spread fast about the quick service and a "gentleman's atmosphere" that resonated from the shop. I intended to keep it that way.

Tanya overheard the guys at the shop talking about the church music I played on Sunday mornings, so she decided to invite me to her church, the First Fruit of God Missionary Baptist Church. I politely declined.

Meanwhile, I was about to break a strict code of mine: dating a girl from the hood, my mother's neighborhood in Highland Park. This girl, Karen, was the complete opposite of what I was looking for in a mate. We both knew it was just a physical thang; well, at least in my mind, it was.

We had sex on the second date. I am talking about butt-naked, stanky, funky, meaningless sex. It was all good, even after a few more sessions of the same, until Karen stopped by the shop unannounced on a busy Saturday afternoon for the first time since we hooked up. She took one look at Tanya, and it was on.

Karen's demeanor turned cold as ice, as she gave me looks that could kill, and made a prompt exit. He instantly made up her mind that I was cheating on her with Tanya, although we were not officially in a relationship.

That's when the obscene calls started pouring into the shop. The cursing and holding the phone and not saying a word; this all had to stop. I cut Karen off with two words, "Go away, bitch." Well, maybe it was three, but who's counting.

No more dates. No more sex. The calls stopped shortly after that, and it was back to business as usual. As it turned out, I would run into Karen at least one more time before she got the message.

After the Karen incident, Tanya would tease me by smiling and shaking her head in silence. We both knew exactly what she was thinking; I just returned the gesture and went about my work.

Tanya wasn't the type to give up so easily, so with a few smiles and a little more persuading, I caved in. What was I thinking?

I cancelled all of my Sunday appointments and attended the First Fruit of God Missionary Baptist Church with my receptionist by my side. I was finally in the house of the Lord, and it wasn't so bad, after all. The preacher was bold in his sermon, and it seemed as though he was preaching directly at me.

Chapter 19

The first stop on my list was Mama's house. In my eyes, she looked completely healthy. The news of our engagement was a bit overwhelming for Mama. "Son, I always knew you would make me proud. Tanya is a God-sent blessing to you, so take care of her and the baby, and God will bless you for that."

"Tanya isn't pregnant, Mama," I said. "We have never even had sex yet."

Mama just nodded her head and said, "I know, baby. I know." Then she fell asleep in her favorite lounge chair. I kissed Mama on her forehead and went about my day.

Tanya and I met for dinner later than evening to discuss plans for the wedding. Over the next few months, the stage was set for our June wedding, and it would be one to remember.

It was the early part of the year, and my brother, Terry, was fresh out of jail and up to his old tricks in the neighborhood. He saw the world as one gigantic pussy waiting to be screwed. Terry hooked up with his old friend, Damon Jacob, who was by then totally addicted to crack cocaine. It was just a matter of time before Terry would join him in that adventure.

In a few months before the wedding, Terry went from strong strapping, good-looking brother to a scrawny, little, dusty-looking crack-head that nobody could trust. On the flip side of my brother's adventures, the wedding plans proceeded on schedule. The church would be decorated in red and white, a theme that Tanya and I chose together. The caterers were on track, and our honeymoon cruise to the Caribbean islands was all paid for. We were simply waiting for June 9th to arrive.

Finally that glorious day came. The First Fruit Missionary Baptist Church was the scene of a blessed and momentous occasion. This would be the sanctuary that witnessed the joining of two very special souls.

I wore a black Armani suit with a white silk tie; that did it for me. No amount of tint could dull the glow that the woman who was to be my wife projected as she stood in the archway of the sanctuary entrance. Tanya was wearing a white pure silk wedding gown; she was waiting to come down the aisle.

My brother stood in as my unofficial best man, which would turn out to be a big mistake, although he would come in handy a few minutes later. Terry was about to make a lasting impression on my new wife and upon our entire church family.

Our wedding was flowing like the gently streaming of a waterfall until the moment the pastor said, "If there is anyone here who opposes the joining of these two souls, speak now or forever hold your peace?"

That's when my old friend, Karen, stood up and spoke her mind. And, boy, did she have plenty to say! She called me everything but a child of God as she stood there in what appeared to be a dirty old wedding dress, reeking of weed, cigarettes, and liquor. She then turned to the lady seated next to her and, with tears in her eyes, said, "This was supposed to be my wedding day."

This girl was really sick in the head and in need of professional help. Terry ran over to her and grabbed her from the back and dragged her out of the church kicking and screaming. The church fell completely silent, as Tanya cried in disappointment at her big day being ruined.

As if that wasn't enough, Terry never returned to the ceremony; instead, he managed to make his way downstairs to the nurse's office, where some of the ladies from the wedding party had stashed their purses for the ceremony. All tolled, Terry made off with four of the ladies' purses and the keys to a brand new Cadillac Seville. I was floored, but more embarrassed for my new wife. After all, this was her church family. I would never see my brother as a free man again.

A month had gone by since our wedding day, and Tanya and I were as happy as two people could be. We moved into our new place at the Jeffersonian Apartments on Jefferson Avenue with plans to buy a new home in a couple of years.

The barbershop was doing extremely well. I had leased 10 of the 12 chairs with one chair remaining. Tanya found a job in the field of social work to match her college degree.

The church was very forgiving and willing to move forward, so we drove to Mama's after service ended. We didn't know, but Mama had been rushed to Henry Ford Hospital in an ambulance with complications to her heart condition. She was placed in the Intensive Care Unit.

Chapter 20

Angel was in the family waiting room crying her eyes out when we arrived at the hospital. My first reaction was fear. Tanya reached for Angel's hand and began to pray. The doctor then entered the waiting room and, speaking only to Angel, said, "We're doing the best we can for your mother. We'll know more over the next 24 hours. We have Mrs. Hardy stabilized, and there is nothing left to do but wait."

When the doctor left the room, that began the most intense moment of my life; things were about to go from bad to worse. The doctors worked tirelessly to save Mama, but despite all their efforts, she would not make it through the night. Alice Hardy died at 3:05 a.m. on a Monday morning of heart complications. She was 65 years old.

Had it not been for the word of God in my life and my precious wife, Tanya, I don't know how I would have made it through that ordeal. Mama's funeral was held at First Fruit MBC, where Pastor W. P. Johns officiated. It was a beautiful going-home celebration.

Tanya sang one of Mama's favorite hymns, "When We All Get to Heaven." The song lifted the spirits of everyone in attendance. It felt as if Mama had passed her comforting and healing hands to my wife. After the hymn, my heart was no longer heavy with grief; I knew my mother was in a better place. Angel took over Mama's house in Highland Park.

Tanya and I prepared to visit her folks down south. We left about four in the morning and drove south on Interstate 75 for about two-and-a-half hours before we decided to pull over for breakfast at a rest stop in Ohio.

Just as we finished our meals, Tanya became nauseous. She ran from the table to the nearest restroom, leaving me and her purse behind. I rushed right behind her with purse in hand. I gently pushed open the door to the ladies room and stuck my head inside, trying not to violate the privacy of other female patrons.

Tanya appeared to be okay as she turned and said she was on her way out. She looked at me with a glowing smile and her watery brown eyes. "Honey, I think I'm pregnant," she exclaimed out loud. I helped her into the car with my mouth stuck on wide open from surprise.

On our next stop for gasoline, we purchased an early pregnancy test kit, and sure enough, Tanya tested positive. We were going to have a baby! My mind immediately went back to what my mother said about Tanya being pregnant. I began to weep for joy and happiness as I embraced my wife like I hadn't seen her for years.

I was joyously elated. We turned the car around and headed back to Detroit, where we would continue to live our lives in peace.

Chapter 21

As for my brother, Terry, God had other plans for his life, as well as for Damon Jacobs. These brothers could get into trouble standing still. Only this time, neither one of them would get the chance to harm another soul.

Damon had convinced the local faggot dealer, R. J., Rocky Jenkins, to let him sell crack from his girlfriend's apartment on Highland Street at the corner of Third in Highland Park. Damon, in turn, brought Terry in to work the other shifts while he and his pregnant girlfriend slept during the day.

Terry was the only person Damon really trusted. They ate, slept, and robbed together, and rarely had any arguments. Terry took his pay in drugs, while Damon had been trying to save money. He even purchased a car so that his girlfriend could get back and forth to her doctor's appointments. Damon Jacobs was trying to get his life back together the best way he knew how.

This didn't set well with Terry, who would help him wreak havoc on unsuspecting people in Detroit, so Terry rounded up a couple of his hard-core junky friends and, with the keys to the apartment, they rushed the unsuspecting dealer. He and his cohorts beat, robbed, and murdered Damon Jacobs for less than $300 in drugs and money. Damon's pregnant girlfriend made the gruesome discovery the next morning after returning from an overnight stay at her sister's place. It took the police nearly two months to catch up with Terry.

Meanwhile, I spotted him in front of the liquor store at Hamilton and Glendale engaged in a heated argument with a strange-looking woman. I had no intention of stopping; I wanted nothing to do with my brother.

Upon Terry's arrest, the police discovered in his possession the set of keys that matched the locks to Damon's girlfriend's apartment. That was all the evidence they needed to seal the fate of my brother. Terry refused to roll over on his accomplices. This so outraged the judge that he sentenced Terry to live without the possibility of parole. Terry Hardy would never again see the light of a free day.

After Mama had passed on, I concentrated my energy on taking care of my wife and the child we were expecting, and my duties to the church. Tanya and I studied our Bibles as if we were in school. I began assisting in Sunday school classes and helping out the devotional services. This made Tanya very proud. She remembered how far I had come since those days on the mean streets of Detroit. These were our better days.

In all of her wisdom and all of her beauty, Tanya was about to add motherhood to that list of precious accolades. I would become a father and an assistant minister at our church. I didn't make a move without consulting my pastor first. He had every confidence in my ability to teach, so he asked me to prepare my trial sermon for the second Sunday of the next month.

I prayed and fasted as I prepared my sermon for that service. The time was close for Tanya to deliver, so she purposely missed the previous Sunday to rest up for what she called my "big day." I had complained of headaches the entire month leading up to my sermon and attributed them to my month-long fast. Finally, the day arrived.

It was the second Sunday at First Fruit MBC where Thomas Hardy, a kid from the mean streets of Detroit, who had seen just about all of the worst things one can imagine, was about to deliver a sermon in front of a congregation of saints and well wishers. Imagine that.

Tanya and Angel sat alongside our pastor and his wife in the front row of pews opposite the Mothers Board. For some strange reason, I was not the least bit nervous.

My sermon was on "Self Destruction", when a man does not know God for himself. The sermon was inspirational and as I was bringing those inspiring words to a close, I came down from the pulpit and stood beneath the podium. "The doors of the church stand open," I said. That was an invitation for anyone to join the church.

At that very moment, a young brother stood up and came forward. I asked him to remove the hood of his sweatshirt while he was in church, and then I asked him his name. That's when he reached down to his belt and pulled out a 9mm handgun and pointed it directly at my chest.

The church fell silent. It was as if everything had frozen, and he and I were the only ones in motion.

"You don't remember me from the barbershop, nigga," he said. "You tried to kill me. Now it's your turn."

At that very moment, a glorious peace and calm came over me and took my mind and spirit to another place. As I began to pray, a warm, illuminating light filled the church, and I began to hear voices shouting and chanting praises unto the Lord. It was like nothing I had experienced before.

I felt myself moving closer to this young man and his gun, until it was pressed firmly against my chest. Then the words of my pastor came out of my mouth, "No weapons formed against me shall prosper. The Lord has led you here this day to be saved, brother, so turn your life over to Him and He will forgive you and your past transgressions."

The young brother dropped his gun and fell to his knees weeping out of control. Brother Marcus was saved that day and is an active member of the First Fruit MBC to this day.

In all the excitement, Tanya's water broke right there in church. The pastor and I rushed her to Children's Hospital, where she gave birth to baby Iyana, which means "one who is loved", and loved she was.

Our lives would never be the same again. Unfortunately, I would live only to see Iyana's third birthday. Those headaches I had complained about stemmed from an aneurysm that managed to rupture. Doctors said that I had gone too long without the proper treatment.

So, on September 16, only days before my 40th birthday, the man you came to know as Thomas Hardy, husband, father, and friend, was no more.

He quietly passed away in his sleep; and his wife, Tanya, never married again.